Dedication

This novel is dedicated to the memory of our family angel, a little boy who's quick whit and love of life inspired me to make him what he always wanted to be:

Strong.....

Thanks for the thousands of buddy kisses.... keep one more for me until we meet again.

© Copyright 2006 McFarlane Media Group
C/O Merdick Earl McFarlane
113 Cranston Road
Providence Bay
Manitoulin Island, Ontario
P0P 1T0

All rights reserved. No part of this publication may be reproduced, stored in a retrieval system, or transmitted, in any form or by any means, electronic, mechanical, photocopying, recording, or otherwise, without the written prior permission of the author.

Note for Librarians: A cataloguing record for this book is available from Library and Archives Canada at www.collectionscanada.ca/amicus/index-e.html
ISBN 1-4251-0886-5

Printed in Victoria, BC, Canada. Printed on paper with minimum 30% recycled fibre.
Trafford's print shop runs on "green energy" from solar, wind and other environmentally-friendly power sources.

Offices in Canada, USA, Ireland and UK

Book sales for North America and international:
Trafford Publishing, 6E–2333 Government St.,
Victoria, BC V8T 4P4 CANADA
phone 250 383 6864 (toll-free 1 888 232 4444)
fax 250 383 6804; email to orders@trafford.com

Book sales in Europe:
Trafford Publishing (UK) Limited, 9 Park End Street, 2nd Floor
Oxford, UK OX1 1HH UNITED KINGDOM
phone +44 (0)1865 722 113 (local rate 0845 230 9601)
facsimile +44 (0)1865 722 868; info.uk@trafford.com

Order online at:
trafford.com/06-2644

10 9 8 7 6 5 4 3

The characters and events in this book are fictitious. Any similarity to real persons, living or dead, is purely coincidental and not intended by the author.

INTRODUCTION

David McAllister, a wealthy and gentrified member of the English aristocracy is also a crusading criminal defense lawyer with a sterling reputation, unlike his reported girl friend Leah Hammond.

One day David receives bad news from his American relatives. His beloved Alicia, a favorite niece has been murdered in New York City. Alicia's brother, David's nephew, is a NYPD detective but even with all of his resources there is no chance to convict the crafty Russian, who is quite adept at covering his tracks. David vows vengeance. He goes to New York and finds Luchensko in an attempt to nail him.

But the Russian is slippery, and to compound matters David McAllister is reported missing in a skiing accident near his villa in Switzerland.

Leah Hammond goes back to New York and again takes up the pursuit of Victor. An attempt to trap him transporting Stinger missiles to Cuba fails and Victor gets away. Leah picks up the Russian's trail in England and through some deductive reasoning figure that Victor is going to smuggle the bomb into the US. Leah had decided to get Victor Luchensko even if it meant killing him in cold blood, but during the adventure she learns something about herself. Rather, she traps him with a combination of female wiles and super intelligence and in the end Victor gets his.

Chapter One

The tall man pushed the silver service teacart into the large dark wood paneling of the mansion's study. His salt and pepper hair belied his stiff ramrod straight bearing. There was nothing subservient about him either, even at this task. He looked more like a British general officer of the Sandhurst variety rather than what he was, a man-servant to Bradley David McAllister, one of England's wealthiest and most colorful barristers. A copy of the *National UK Observer* was on the tray along with the scones and tea accouterments.

McAllister, a slim, handsome and urbane man, looked up from the documents he had been perusing at his large mahogany desk. The desk was one of the few concessions to the modern time. A scan of the room suggested the essence of another time, a time of Arthur, Lancelot and Guinevere, a time when honor and loyalty and friendship were the most important things in life. These things were the heart and soul of David McAllister.

Any Knight of the Realm would have been at home here. The walls were adorned with crossed broadswords, battle axes, lances and flanking the fireplace was a suit of armor from head to toe. The walls also displayed various awards earned by David in the martial arts. There were certificates of black belts, brown belts and full regalia of both Karate and Tae Kwan Do.

While David McAllister obviously ascribed to some kind of warrior code, paradoxically, he was one of those males so finely and delicately featured that his face could be construed as beautiful.

Albert pushed the tea service cart up to a side table. David said, "Ah, Albert, afternoon tea, the last refuge of the truly civilized eh?" He was grinning as he spoke.

But Albert remained rather stoic and professional. He said, "I brought you the *Observer,* sir. As you asked," he added as if to make clear that it certainly wasn't his own idea.

Albert poured the tea and David began to stir some sugar into his cup. As he sipped he glanced at the front page of the *Observer.* Albert was still busy when David muttered, "So it's true. Leah has gotten into a sticky wicket again."

Albert looked up. "Sir?"

"You didn't read this?"

"No, sir. As you know I prefer the *Daily News.*"

"That woman has an absolute talent for offending the wrong people. Seems that some rowdy tourists spotting her at the Elegant Club, made some comments about her rather unique disco dancing style and she wound up clocking one of them."

"Oh dear," Albert said, "I hope she wasn't arrested."

"She most certainly was. She was lucky to be booked by one of my detective friends. He saw to it that she went straight to the flat in Piccadilly and told her to stay out of trouble for a while." With a grin David said, "I believe she will for a fortnight or two."

"I hope so, sir, for your sake. She gets in so much trouble it could be a problem for all of us."

Albert's brows tended to knit together and David presupposed his question. "I just wanted to see how much of a snit the Observer made of it."

Fussing with the tray Albert asked, "And did they?"

"Oh for sure. Here it is," David said pointing to an article under a picture of a beautiful young woman appearing to be shouting at someone. "Miss Leah Hammond, the lady friend of London's most famous barrister, Bradley David McAllister."

"Ah, trust the *Observer* to exaggerate and to embellish."

"Well, in Leah's case they may embellish but they certainly are not exaggerating. That woman can find trouble in a convent."

"I believe she will stay out of trouble for a while. I only wish you would go out once in while and not leave all the fun up to Miss Hammond."

"I kind of enjoy it this way, Albert."

Shifting gears Albert said, "Do you wish me to call you for dinner, sir?"

"No. Just bring me a plate here in the study."

Albert nodded, and departed.

Later that evening Albert tapped lightly on the study door. David was busy with some paperwork. He called for Albert to come in but did not look up from his papers until he sensed Albert standing in front of him. When he looked up he saw trouble in the pale blue eyes of his man-servant. They had been together for over fifteen years and knew each other well. David was certain something was wrong. "Sir," Albert said, and paused.

"What is it, Albert? I heard the phone."

"It's terrible news from America, sir."

David put his papers aside and took a deep breath signaling to Albert that he was ready for this bad news.

It was not customary for Albert to stammer so when he started out and he did stammer, David knew this was truly bad.

Albert said, "It was your sister-in-law Brenda. She has informed us of the sad news that your niece Alicia has been murdered."

David said nothing but stared at Albert. A moment later he dropped his head into his hands as he heard Albert move off somewhere. When he looked up Albert had a decanter of brandy in hand and said, "May I pour you a glass, sir?"

"Yes, thank you, Albert." He remained quiet while Albert poured. Then he said, "Pour yourself one if you wish, Albert.'

"Thank you, sir," he said as he handed David the drink and poured himself one.

David sipped his drink and stared into the fire in the fireplace before speaking. "Brenda didn't wish to speak to me?"

"No, sir. She was very upset and I got the impression that she just wanted me to inform you."

"Damn it, Albert, I loved that girl. But Brenda remains bitter with me. She still believes I should have done more to save my dear brother from his troubles and his eventual demise. She doesn't believe that my brother, her Alicia and Jonathan are all the family I have and that I love them all dearly. Her bitterness towards me is painful."

"Yes indeed, sir, I know."

"As for Alicia, I tried everything I could think of to keep her off her dangerous path. Do you remember the time we had her over here?"

"Yes, sir," Albert said, sipping on his own drink. "I became quite fond of the young lady myself. It's too bad we couldn't keep her here longer."

"Ah yes," David said, the sadness coating his words in a hoarse whisper, on the verge of tears "If only we could have kept her interested in the life of a country lady. But she was intent on her tumultuous life in the city."

Albert asked, "You mean her night life, sir?"

"Yes. She had a penchant for the club scene. A lot like our Leah."

"Ah, yes, sir. That's true."

"As for the rest of the McAllister family tragedy my dear sister in law still blames me for my brother's misfortune in losing his share of the McAllister fortune."

"Hasn't she and her son, Jonathan, been able to retain some of the money?"

"Yes, but of course it is only a fraction of the fortune my brother had inherited."

The two were quiet for a moment, only the steady ticking of the grandfather clock filling the room. Finally, David said, "I suppose Brenda didn't stay on the phone long enough to give you any details of Alicia's murder, or whether or not the New York police have any leads.'

"No, sir. You are right there. Although she did say that they suspected some Russian Mafia gangster in New York."

"I know the one. In my efforts to keep an eye on my niece I have learned of her involvement with one Victor Luchensko. He is the one you are referring to."

"Oh dear," Albert said and took another sip of his drink.

"Albert, would you get me onto tomorrow evening's flight to New York City? I have some estate planning to do which I will discuss with you before I leave."

"Yes, sir. I will look to it immediately." He hesitated. "As to this estate planning, sir, from our conversations I know what you are planning, but... but do you think that is the best way to handle things?"

David leveled a gaze from his steely gray eyes at Albert. "Yes, Albert, I know it's the right thing to do."

Stepping back in an obedient manner, the white haired man said, "Yes. Very well, sir. Whatever you wish."

Chapter Two

David was sitting in the dim light of the study. He scanned the room and the objects in it. Things that once had been dear to him. Things he cherished, like the pipe set on his desk that his father had given him. But now they just seemed to be things and he was anxious to be away from them. It was early afternoon and the lowering sun was casting long shadows that crept across the Oriental rugs. He was still deep in thought so was startled a bit by the tap on the door. "Come on in, Albert." Albert had a stack of manila folders under his arm.

"Would you like to go over the estate arrangements?" he asked.

"Just the basics, Albert. I'm sure you were thorough. And relax. You look so tense."

"Well it is a trying time, sir."

"I know, Albert, but today is your last official day as my employee. Could we have a drink together?"

"Oh yes. That would be fine."

As he started for the sideboard, David motioned him to a chair. "Sit. I'll get the drinks. Only a splash of vermouth in your martini?"

"Yes, sir. That would be fine."

"I'm no longer, *Sir* to you, Albert."

The older man looked flustered. "Oh I'm sorry, s.... I mean, David. Years of habit are hard to break."

David managed a weak smile. "Yes. How long has it been? About fifteen years now?" He handed Albert his drink. "Here. I believe it's the way you like it." As Albert accepted it David raised his glass and said, "Here's to better times."

"Well, I hope so, sir. I just wish that you didn't have to dispose of all your property so quickly. The deal on the estate in Munich that we sold to your friend was particularly unfair, bit of a steal." He quickly amended his words. "A steal for him, a bad deal for you."

"And the London property?"

"All taken care of, sir. And as you wish all evidence of you and your residence will have been removed. In fact," he said sifting through the folders, "here is the deed and paperwork transferring the estate to Leah Hammond's name. This will take effect in three weeks as you requested and also the paperwork is there for you to sign authorizing my solicitors to turn the proceeds of this estate over to my account in Geneva once the deal is finalized. The last thing you requested, sir, is all evidence of your residence in your estates will be removed before all transactions are finalized."

Albert sipped his drink and sighed. "It's too bad about the financial losses though."

David gazed at him from a moment. "I'm looking at my life differently now, Albert, I now have a purpose. My first will be to take care of that vile creature in New York, that Russian criminal who killed Alicia. And then it will be on to a new life for me."

"And what about the Yew York hotel property, sir?"

"That property will be left to Leah Hammond as well along with the funds from the Munich estate sale. I have made the necessary changes in my will, which I finalized last night. I also left my nephew Jonathan and his mother Brenda enough money to get by on should something happen to me."

"I understand, sir. But is all this truly necessary?" His face twisted into a small grimace. "I mean...And then there is the money loss, it still..."

David interrupted, seeking to change the subject. "Hush, Albert. Who is it....Cervantes, I think, who said, 'The gratification of wealth is not found in mere possessions or in lavish expenditures but in its wise application.'"

"I suppose, sir," he said, still looking unconvinced.

"I do want to thank you for your help, Albert. Your loyalty will never be forgotten. You are going ahead with me on my plans knowing that one misstep could land us in Wormswood for years."

"Indeed, sir."

David had to grin at the lapse and return to protocol. "Actually I've said goodbye to this house after my brother Keith left for the States. His financial missteps and failure followed by his suicide have left me as bitter as his wife Brenda and his son Jonathan in some way."

"But it wasn't your fault, sir."

"That's true but only in a technical sense, Albert."

"Sir?"

"It is kind of a sin by omission. I knew he was having difficulties, but he is my older brother and I guess I expected him to bail himself out. But instead look what happened."

"He was...well...he was not suited, shall we say to handle a lot of money. That's not your fault. Some people, like yourself, have a knack for handling wealth. Others do not. I don't see it as a weakness. Then there are always the vagaries and ups and downs of the financial world. It could have happened to anyone."

"Again, Albert, you're right but only in one sense. I feel I should have seen his distress and lent a helping hand before disaster struck. And in my brother Keith's case it was indeed his fault. I didn't want to interfere. It would hurt his pride. But I did see him or rather I sensed he was moving in the wrong direction. I should have helped him."

Albert sipped his martini before speaking. "I think you are wrong, sir, he was too stubborn, too proud to accept advice on business matters from his younger brother. I believe if you so much as tried to help he would have rejected it."

David continued sipping his own drink. "You may be right, Albert, but nevertheless I still feel guilty about it. And I feel strongly that I should uphold the family honor and take care of this Luchensko fellow for the murder of Alicia." He sipped his drink thoughtfully. "I often wondered why she would get involved with such a type of man."

Albert sighed. "Some young women are attracted to dangerous fellows like him, sir. They see them not as evil but some sort of dashing rogue." Albert lapsed quiet. When he spoke his voice was grim. "He's a dangerous one, sir. His main business is narcotics and he is heavily involved with the Cartagena cartel. Our intelligence reports that although he has not been convicted, nay, not even charged it is thought that he is responsible for the demise of at least a half dozen beautiful young women. And he is difficult if not impossible to get near since he never travels without a phalanx of bodyguards, vicious thugs, all. With that kind of backing he is able to indulge in his penchant for beautiful young women."

David was back quickly. "And that will be his downfall, Albert. That is how we are going to get him."

"Sir?"

"Beautiful women are his Achilles' heel. That's what will betray his cunning."

Albert now seemed reconciled to David's intentions.

After a bit more silence David asked, "Am I all set for my flight this evening?"

"Yes, sir. You are booked in First Class on British Airways to New York. I have arranged for a car and a hotel room for you in New York as well. The limo service will transport you to Heathrow."

David locked eyes with Albert. The older man looked sad. David said, "Everything comes to an end, Albert. No need to be sad."

"I guess so, sir. I guess I just hate change."

"Something is over and something else is about to begin. That's something to be happy about. New things should make one happy."

David finished his drink. Albert did likewise and rose from his chair. "Well, sir, it is very difficult to say goodbye and I will miss being your number one man and…friend."

David's smile was warm and genuine. "You will never stop being that, Albert. Not ever."

Chapter Three

The British Airways 777 cruised quietly at 30,000 feet over the wine dark Atlantic. David sat in the First Class cabin sipping a Manhattan and thinking. Most of his thoughts were about his niece, Alicia. The young woman had held a special place in his heart. And right now he was thinking about why. What did he have in common with the young woman that had made her so special to him? Of course, she had been special to her mother and brother, Jonathan too. She was a fine girl. If not for her penchant for a rare combination of independence, rebelliousness and curiosity she might be alive today instead of laying in a coffin at a Manhattan funeral parlor.

David remembered the time he had taken her trout fishing at his lodge in the Scottish highlands. She was a fast learner and truly loved the sport, learning to cast the fly out effortlessly and then trolling it gently along the likely hiding spots of the trout. David found himself trying harder than ever to catch trout. She was genuine competition and of course it was Alicia who had the first strike. The trout was a monster and David thought for sure it was the one called "Old Wally" which fishermen had been trying to catch for years. Alicia played the fish as if she had been trout fishing all her life. The enormous size of this fish made him especially difficult to land. Whenever David tried to assist her she insisted she could handle it. And she did. A couple of passing fishermen stopped to watch. Everyone was sure she had "Old Wally." A legend would end right here today at this trout stream. The locals were a bit jealous that they had been trying for years to catch this fish and this whippet of an English lass had out fished them all. As Alicia held the fish in her net, a couple of the locals took a picture. He still had it today on his mantle. But a tear came to Alicia's eye as she watched the great fish struggle in the net. Quickly and gently, she removed the hook, inserted a finger in his gill and threw him back into the river. A gasp went up from the assembled Scots. "Why'd you do that, Lass. You have "Old Wally" the biggest toughest trout of them all."

Alicia caught David's eyes. "He's so beautiful, so free, I couldn't take his life just so I could say 'I caught "Old Wally."'"

David smiled, proud of her. "You make me proud, girl."

He hugged her and she wept softly. Looking up at him she said, "Do you think me the fool?"

"God no, girl. I think you're the finest human being I've ever known."

He never forgot the incident and he knew it was what made Alicia special to him. And he knew she felt the same.

Whoever had harmed her. Whoever had killed her was going to pay. He had made this vow the minute he heard she had been murdered.

He dozed off with his mortal thoughts and was awakened by the rattle of breakfast trays, the smell of coffee and the sun slanting in his window.

By the time the plane landed with a thump, a squeal of rubber and the roar of reverse thrusting engines, David was burning with a steely resolve, a burning desire to kill that miserable Russian, or whomever he found out was responsible for Alicia's death.

He was whisked off through the Manhattan traffic to his hotel on the

Upper East Side. When he checked in he asked, "Is Ms Leah Hammond in the hotel?"

The clerk, recognizing him said, "Not yet sir. But she left a message for you early this morning saying she would check in around three this afternoon. Would you like to leave a message?"

"No. That's fine. I'll catch up with her later."

Later, David appeared in casual clothes, went outside into the bright sunshine and the doorman hailed him a cab. He told the driver, "Lou's Gym. It's over in the Bowery on Hudson Avenue. Do you know it?"

The driver cast a glance at him. "Sure. Thing is, are you sure you want to go down there?"

David smiled. "I'm sure."

Lou's was in a section of the Bowery that was even more run down and seedy then the rest of the area. Several businesses on the street were boarded up. Trash and beer cans littered the gutters. David handed the driver a twenty and carrying a gym bag, he alighted. The sign out in front was faded and peeling. If one was careful the words, Karate, Tai Kwan Do and Aikodo could be read. He went inside. The driver, watching, gave a kind of roll of the eyes.

A wiry little bald headed man at the desk looked up from his crossword. "Hey there, David. Nice to see you. Are we your first stop of the day?"

"Yes, Lou. I'd rather do some Karate than run like most normal people. Is there anybody around who might like to work out with me?"

Lou grinned. "There's usually some here by ten. But you're going to have to get somebody who doesn't know you."

David feigned ignorance. "I beg our pardon?"

"Well, you wiped the floor with the last ones. So you need fresh meat. Why don't you go warm up and I'll let you know if some worthy opponent comes in."

David changed into his Karate outfit, white robe and pants with a neutral colored sash. He was slight of build and not particularly impressive. When Lou came in hiding a little grin he had a large fierce looking guy with him. He was cue ball bald and it was obvious that his nose had been broken at least a few times. When he caught sight of David doing some stretching exercises he turned to Lou. "Are you kidding me?"

"What?" Lou said innocently. "He's a pro I'm telling you. Don't let that slight build fool you."

The bald guy shook his head. "Look. I don't want to be charged with murder. I just want to work out. This guy is pretty enough to be a broad."

Lou said, "Don't let his small build fool you. He's fast. As a matter of fact I'll lay odds, ten to one that he strikes the first blow."

The big guy's grin revealed small stumps of yellowish teeth. "Come on, Lou. You in love with this guy? You're willing to bet money?"

"American dollars."

"He lands the first hit."

"Right."

"Okay. You're on. I like easy money."

Lou introduced the two. "David, this is Bruno. Bruno, David."

David stuck out his hand and Bruno did his best to give a hard enough squeeze to elicit a wince from most men. But David simply smiled at him.

When the two got in the ring, the difference between them was shocking. David looked like a Preppy in a hobo camp.

The opponents faced each other and went through the ancient rituals of respect an honor. David particularly loved this part of the sport. He deeply respected the rituals and the ancient principles behind them. While David bowed deeply and respectfully, his opponent went through the motions in a superficial and callous manner.

The two strode casually around each other eying each other like prey. If one was the wolf the other was the lamb. Bruno kept grinning and David maintained a pleasant if not jovial demeanor. David took the side facing straddle stance called *sesan dachi* because he felt that it intimidated a larger opponent like Bruno. First all of his limbs used for striking were not in view in this stance and secondly he felt viewing the man from a peripheral stance put him off balance. Suddenly, David stopped, whirled and landed an in place kick on Bruno's jaw. He fended off the inevitable counter thrust with a backhand block called *ura uke*. Bruno staggered back, more surprised than hurt. He wiped a bit of blood off his mouth and looked at David, incredulous. Bruno tried another blow, this one blocked by an open hand block called a *shotei otoshi uke*. Lou grinned. But Bruno never looked at the little gym owner. His first impulse was to rush David. That was a mistake. David stopped him with a flurry of hand and elbow jabs, the last one to the back of his neck sending the big man crashing to the mat.

As Bruno on hands and knees shook himself like a wet dog, David, very calmly strode around and waited for him to get up. He decided not to. Even though the victor, David bowed low in respect to a worthy opponent.

Word got around the gym and opponents, now eager to prove themselves, began showing up. David made short work of them and when he was done was satisfied that he had a good work-out.

Back at the hotel David indulged in a heavier than usual lunch since he had burned up so many calories at the gym. He dined on a nice grilled piece of halibut, Delmonico potatoes and a large Caesar salad. For dessert he indulged in a piece of German Bavarian chocolate cake he had learned to love from his life in Switzerland.

After lunch he changed into more formal attire and took a cab to the 22nd Precinct in Manhattan and a meeting with his nephew Jonathan, a gold shield with NYPD. David confirmed that Jonathan was available before he left.

An hour later he was sitting in front of Jonathan's desk. Behind him were some family pictures and David saw his brother Keith in several pictures in happier days. There was also a picture or two of Alicia.

Jonathan was happy to see his uncle but beneath the exterior smile he was deeply sad. David said, "I'm so sorry, Jonathan. I loved that girl as if she was my own."

"I know, Uncle David. I know. She was headstrong. Wouldn't listen to anybody. Still…"

"Still she didn't deserve what she got at the hands of that monster. Are we still sure it was him?"

Jonathan sighed. "We're sure in the sense of it doesn't seem likely it was anybody else or that it was a random murder. As you know, the trouble is this guy is heavy duty Mafia. He protects himself from every quarter. He has some of the biggest politicians in Albany in his pocket. Of course I couldn't prove any of that. In fact I'm having enough trouble convincing anyone that I have enough evidence for an indictment."

"So the investigation isn't going well."

Jonathan said, "I'm afraid if we have to rely on the law we aren't going to get him. His trail is clean."

"So…You're saying that…"

"Keep that speculation to yourself, Uncle. All I'm saying is that in my position, I'm going to have a tough time developing any evidence against him."

"I see."

"Do you? Do you realize that he can get any number of politicians or other VIPs to say he was with them as an alibi? I've never seen a hood so well protected."

"I know how it is, Jonathan. I've done enough in my own practice with people in high places who protect people like this Russian. It's because of his funding. He has so much money, there is hardly anybody that he can't bribe."

David had the picture. He now wanted to breach another subject. "Jonathan, please don't argue with me on this. I want to pay for Alicia's funeral and I want to spare no expense."

Jonathan sighed and tapped his fingers on his desk. "I dunno, Uncle. You know how my mother is. I…"

"I can't say I really know how your mother is, Jonathan, but I do know this. Somewhere deep down she doesn't really blame me for Keith's problems. I might have been able to do more but in this life no man is his brother's keeper. Everybody shifts for themselves and if one needs help he should ask. Keith never asked. If it is my responsibility for not asking remember this. Keith is my older brother. He wasn't used to taking charity from his kid brother. So as I said, deep down, I don't think your mother really blames me. One day she will realize that."

"I hope you are right."

David leveled a gaze at his nephew. "Jonathan, I want to help you catch this Russian but if we can't bring him to justice I am telling you this unofficially, I am going to get him."

"How, Uncle? He is powerful and is surrounded by some dedicated bodyguards."

"Leave that to me, Jonathan. I don't want to advocate vigilante justice but I swear to you that this monster will not get away with this."

Jonathan allowed a rather wry grin cross his face. "I know how you feel but I represent authority and law here. I would like to get him too but I can't even contemplate it. In fact I'm lucky the boss hasn't taken me off the case already because of my closeness to it. But while I'm on the case I'll give you any information that you think you can use. It's true. You could do things that the police can't."

He lapsed silent for a moment. Only the office clatter broke the silence between them. Jonathan then said, "I don't want you to get into any trouble over this. This scumbag isn't worth it."

"I need to do what I need to do, Jonathan. Don't worry about me."

Chapter Four

Leah had dressed very carefully this evening. She applied her makeup skillfully accentuating her high cheekbones. While she showed a lot of leg, up top she had selected clothes that were not revealing or risqué. All in all her outfit was ultra chic. She was wearing David's mother's diamond necklace she got from the London apartment.

Now she was outside the hotel. Dusk was falling as the wind kicked up whitecaps on the mighty Hudson River and then whistled down the canyons of the West Side of Manhattan. Leah was standing in front of her hotel as the sharp breeze wrapped her coat around her and fanned her gorgeous long hair out.

The doorman approached her, tipped his cap and asked, "Can I get you a cab, ma'am?"

She smiled. "No. Thank you but I have a limo coming."

Just then a long white stretch limo appeared and parked. Before the driver could come around the doorman opened the door and Leah flashed him a smile and swung her sleek, long limbs into the car with a whisper of silk.

Leah stretched out in the dark cavern of the limo and gazed out at the flow and ebb of New York City traffic, which at this time of day was mostly in the ebb. She was deep in thought.

In a matter of two hours Leah had been in and out of three of the trendiest disco clubs in the City, including Studio 54. She had done some dancing in each of them but didn't look in the least tired.

Eventually the limo pulled up in front of Mandy's, one of Manhattan's newest most chic, by invitation only, nightclubs. There was a line that stretched around the block and every head turned at the sight of the limo. Since Mandy's was a haven for celebrities of all kinds the crowd focused on the long car to see who was arriving. The driver got out, had a word with the doorman, shook his hand and returned to the car. He opened the rear door. "It's OK, Ms. Hammond. You can go in."

"Thanks, Charles."

"I will be right here when you come out. If I have to move around the block, just use your cell to let me know."

The place was other-worldly. The dance floor was packed with dancers, their drugged out faces bathed in strobe lights of every color, their bodies writhing like they were in the throes of some ancient ceremonial tribal dance. The lights, the bodies and the pounding, primal beat of the music all combined for a sense of the surreal.

Leah was led to a table. When seated she crossed her legs, her mini revealing a flash of thigh and ordered a Gray Goose Vodka Martini.

Across the room Victor Luchensko was enjoying the scene, drinking and cavorting with a bevy of beautiful young Manhattanites.

Leah averted her gaze but Luchensko did not. From time to time he would gaze over at her. A beautiful woman, alone, she was soon asked by several doting males to dance, which she did.

Victor could not take his eyes off her as she danced. She had a style that was akin to the Hawaiian hula dancer. Limp wrists on hips she rotated and bumped with an abandon that had Victor's eyes glued to her hips. Every once in a while she would cast a coquettish smile his way but not directly at him.

After the dance her partner asked her to have a drink at the bar with him. She accepted. As one of the busy bartenders caught sight of her he nudged his co-worker. "Who's the fox?"

"Don't know. She's not one of the regulars."

As his partner poured a drink he said, "Look at the Russian. He looks like he'd like to have her for dinner."

"Yeah. She's a little old by his standards, but I can't fault his judgment."

As Leah was drinking with her gentleman friend, a waiter arrived with a drink for her. He had to almost shout above the noise as he motioned to Victor. "From the gentleman, ma'am."

"Please thank the gentleman and tell him, I've had my fill for the evening."

"Yes, ma'am," the harried waiter said as he worked his way back through the crowd to Victor's table.

Leah watched the waiter talk to him. The tall, urbane Russian with the neatly trimmed black mustache and goatee turned to her, saluted her with his champagne glass and smiled. The gesture was unmistakable and said, " another time."

When she finished her drink, Leah thanked her escort and headed for the door. A young man from Victor's table also got up and followed her. The limo was waiting. The driver already had the door open as she made for it. Once inside, she said, "Charles, let's take a spin around the Park. It's a nice night and I love New York at night."

"Yes, ma'am," he said, as he eased the long car away from the curb.

The young man stood on the sidewalk, his eyes glued to the limos license plate. Then he went back inside.

The skyline of Manhattan sparkled like diamonds in the black velvet night as Leah gazed from her comfortable perch. She thought, *what would the world be without New York City? There's nowhere like this town.*

When she got to her hotel room door she spotted a dozen red roses leaning up against it. She picked them up and plucked off the card.

It read, "Sleep tight, beautiful lady." It wasn't signed, but Leah had no doubts about it.

How had he found my hotel so quickly? And how did he get my name?

You have to give it to him. He really works fast.

Leah knew that she had to play him just right. If she were too eager she would lose the advantage that she needed. She had to lure him like a trout hungry for the bait she was using. True he was one of the biggest, most evil trout in the stream, but that was all more the reason to play him right.

She was getting ready for bed when the phone rang. It was Victor Luchensko. "Ms Hammond?"

"Yes."

"It is Victor Luchensko. We met at Mandy's this evening."

"We did?"

"Yes. I sent you the drink. You were at the bar with a gentleman."

"Oh! That was you!"

"Yes."

"And the roses too?"

"Yes, guilty again."

Something about the way he said, 'guilty' rankled her but she kept controlled. "How did you get my address?"

"A determined man can find almost anything."

She could almost see that grin he had displayed in Mandy's. "I guess so."

He lapsed a bit more serious. "I know that I should have made a more formal introduction or asked someone to do it for me. I am really Old World at heart."

"I see."

"I don't think you do. You see, I think you are the most beautiful woman I have ever seen."

"That sounds like a real compliment since you undoubtedly have known many beautiful women."

She could see the grin again. "You are so right."

"Well, thank you for the compliment, Mr. Luchensko…………."

He interrupted, "Victor please. We have now been introduced."

"Okay. Victor."

He said, "I would like to invite you to lunch tomorrow. The Russian Tea Room? Say 1:30?"

"I don't know…I…"

"Please don't break my heart, Ms Hammond."

Leah deliberately hesitated. After a dozen heartbeats she said, "I suppose you wouldn't have your uh…entourage around for an intimate lunch at the Russian Tea Room?"

"Of course not. This evening was a kind of boys' night out. A celebration. One of my uh…staff was getting married. No. I can assure you it will be just you and I."

"If I say yes you will have to meet a couple of my conditions."

"And they are?"

"First, that we proceed, that is if we proceed, at my pace. Second, if I say no at any point, that is final. I don't intend to be fighting you off if I decide I am not interested."

"Fair enough. You are so forceful. A woman who knows what she wants. It is so rare. I'm not used to that."

There was a pause as though he expected some cute or caustic remark. In fact she had contemplated one but since she didn't really know him she had no idea how he'd react. She didn't want to let him off the hook.

"Okay, then. The Russian Tea Room at 1:30."

"I so look forward to it."

There was a pause as if he expected her to chorus his remark. Instead she said, "See you then."

She hung up and gazed out the window for a while. A smile played across her beautiful face.

Chapter Five

David was up early. After a breakfast of coffee, juice and a croissant he headed for the front desk where he wrote Leah a note and handed it to the desk clerk. "Would you see that Ms Hammond gets this?"

"Certainly sir, I don't think I've seen her yet this morning."

Outside, David had a limo waiting. It took a half hour in the morning traffic to reach the funeral home, which was on the Upper East Side. He took a deep breath and composed himself before he got out of the limo.

As he entered the establishment the sickening sweet smell of flowers greeted him. His heart thumped harder. He was met in the lobby by his nephew, Jonathan. He held out his arms and the younger man embraced him. Emotions were high. Murmuring into his shoulder, David said, "Good morning, Jonathan. How are you under the circumstances?"

"I'm OK, Uncle. I've come to grips with my sister's death. I wish I could say the same for my mother."

"Is she here?"

"Yes. We were just told that Alicia's body wouldn't be ready for viewing until tomorrow."

"Why is that?"

"The Department is still trying to get as much trace evidence as possible. I have to say it is some of my doing. We need all the evidence we can find. The wake is being delayed until tomorrow. Anything to help us catch this killer."

His voice hard, David said, "Yes. Except we, know who killed her."

Jonathan bit his lip. "I know, Uncle. But I can't go off being a vigilante on this. I'm a member of the Department and I, especially, have to go by the book."

Just then Brenda appeared from another room. When she spotted David she hesitated. David approached her. "Hello, Brenda. I wish we could be meeting under different circumstances." The woman nodded solemnly and the three walked into the nearest lounge and took seats facing one another. David's eyes were red. Jonathan's too.

Brenda said, "I know what you mean and I do too, David. I want you to know that regardless, I appreciate your help with Alicia's final expenses."

David said, "I wish there wasn't a need for you to use the term, regardless."

Brenda said, "I am a bitter woman, David. I won't go as far as to say I'm vindictive. The practical side of me understands that you are not the only reason why my late husband fell so low, still I…"

Jonathan interrupted. "Mother. I believe I know Father as well as anyone and it was his own stubborn pride that caused his downfall. He could have asked Uncle David for help but he chose not to. By the time anyone really knew about his financial troubles it was too late. It's wrong to hold Uncle David responsible."

Brenda offered only a cold, stony silence.

David said, "It hurts me, Brenda, that you and Jonathan and I can't be more family at a time like this. I'm only grateful that my brother is not here to see what has happened to his little girl." The silence now grew deeper and lasted more than a dozen heartbeats.

Then Jonathan dropped his face into his hands. A small sob broke the silence.

David said, "Brenda, whatever you think about the state of our family's affairs, I loved that girl like she was my own."

Brenda took a deep breath. So softly, it could hardly be heard she said, "I know that David. I know."

David said, "And furthermore, I intend to see that justice is done with or without the help of the NYPD."

Jonathan looked up. He said, "Uncle..."

Now David interrupted as he stood. "I'll see you two at the wake tomorrow. Be kind to each other." With that he was out the door to his waiting limo.

The traffic had abated somewhat and they arrived at Lou's gym within the hour. There was nobody around for a match so David contented himself with a strenuous workout and an inordinate amount of time on the punching bag. He was glistening with sweat and panting when he finally quit.

After a shower he got back in the limo and headed uptown for lunch. He was pleasantly tired and relaxed at the same time. Gazing out the window at the passing magnificence of Fifth Avenue he was distracted by the buzzing of the limo phone. It was Albert. David listened and then said, "Yes, the arrangements your friend made. I understand. Thanks for calling, Albert."

David then directed the driver to make a turn around somewhere and reverse direction. Lunch wouldn't be uptown after all.

David entered the club. It was appropriately dark and extravagantly elegant. Sporting the décor of a turn of the century New York Men's club it was a world of palm fronds, shined brass and polished mahogany. There were even shiny brass spittoons spotted around. He sought out the maitre de, was told there were no tables available, tipped him generously and was led to a table near Victor Luchensko and his entourage.

He dined lightly on broiled scrod and asparagus, which he washed down with an excellent white wine from the Rhineland. While he didn't make eye contact with Victor the Russian was never out of his sight.

David kept his prey under surveillance like a lioness at the edge of a herd of antelope. He was interested in learning more about this Russian gangster. It didn't take him long to decide that there was nothing unique or special about him. He flirted with the waitresses and made eyes at other attractive women whether they were escorted or not. The thought flashed through the Englishman's mind. *What in the world did my little Alicia see in this shallow man? What was she searching for when she decided on this poor excuse for a human being?*

David timed his lunch to end just as the Russian seemed about to leave. He wiped his lips with a napkin and approached the gangster. As he did, a phalanx of bodyguards positioned themselves around him. David held his ground and did not move, impeding their advance. Victor cast an arrogant glance at the foppish looking Englishman. David was dressed more like an English country squire than a New Yorker and it seemed to amuse Victor.

David said, "I need to speak to you, sir!"

"Do we know each other?"

David leveled his gaze on him. "Not yet, sir."

"What do we have to talk about?"

David's eyes narrowed into a glare. Luchensko didn't miss it. "What's on your mind, Mr. ... Uuuhh."

"McAllister. David McAllister."

"McAllister, hmmmm," he said, stroking his chin.

"Yes, like in Alicia McAllister. I am her uncle."

"I don't know any ...what is it, Lisa McAllister?"

As David went for his wallet in his inside breast coat pocket the bodyguards stiffened and also reached into their coats.

David quickly retrieved his wallet. "Tell your men to calm down. After all, there are three of them and only one of me."

Victor smirked even as David handed him a photo. "This is Alicia McAllister. Do you remember her now?"

The Russian gave the photo a cursory glance and handed it back. "No,

I don't know this lady. Why? Should I?"

"I intend to make sure you not only remember her but never forget her."

The Russian's smirk morphed into an evil grin. "And you are going to do that to me, little man?"

David had an evil smile of his own. "Oh don't put too much emphasis on size, my friend. Remember David and Goliath of the Bible. You know how that turned out. That is I assume you have heard of the Bible?"

The smile disappeared from Victor's face. "Yes I have heard about it. But maybe you put too much hope in it and its fables."

"Fables?" David said with a lift of a brow. "I've never heard that reference to the Bible before. Well," he continued, "I'd say, beware of fables. They could come true. Good day, sir." Satisfied with having the last word he left the little group slack jawed.

Dusk was falling as David, now in the slums of the lower East Side, entered a parking garage and as if directed made his way to the third level tier and headed for a specific car. The door was unlocked. He reached in and found the keys on the floor under the front seat. He then opened the glove compartment and retrieved a dark manila folder. Sorting through it he found a motel key. It was on a triangular red tag with the Room Number 101 and the name, *Downtown Motel* was printed on it. He started the engine and drove out of the garage.

An hour later he pulled up in front of a rundown motel. The letters *w* and *n* were out on its neon sign and the parking lot looked like it hadn't been swept in a month. Beer cans and litter were everywhere.

He climbed the outside stairs and headed for Room 101, used his key and entered. It was a typical cheap motel. Cinder block walls painted a muted green, long ago faded. Curtains that hung limply and hadn't seen a pressing in a year, a shag rug rich with unidentifiable stains, a lumpy bed and a TV that had seen better days. The bathroom area was much the same.

On the bed, neatly laid out, were women's clothes. The fine clothes and the neat arrangement mocked the dumpy motel room and seemed as out of place as a preppy in a hobo camp. Deep in thought, David ran his fingers lightly over them as if they were precious mementos of another, a better time.

He wandered to the window, parted the curtain and peered out into the gaudily lit street. He was in an area of motels, liquor stores and junk shops that sold everything from cameras to switch blade knives. Eventually he seemed to gain purpose and turned back into the room.

Chapter Six

Leah dabbed her lips with the crisp white linen napkin. The service at the Russian Tea Room was as efficient and unobtrusive as usual as it moved smoothly about her and Victor who were in the middle of lunch. The conversation so far has been mundane but Leah had dropped a few loaded questions which if answered, would prove revealing. But Victor, as wary as a fox, played the game with caution. So far she learned only what he wanted her to know and that wasn't much more than he was a rich Russian businessman. With a penchant for beautiful women.

Victor raised his wine glass to his lips, peered at her over the rim and smiling, said, "So tell me. After so much resistance what made you decide to change your mind and go out with me?"

With a coy smile of her own, she gazed back at him and didn't answer right away. Then, "Shall we say curiosity?"

The grin that played around the edges of his mouth took on the characteristics of a smirk.

Though smiling, Leah was irritated. There was something about unbridled arrogance that she could not abide.

He said, "You know what they say about curiosity?"

"You mean about it killing the cat?"

"Yes."

"First of all I'm smarter than a cat." And now wearing her own Cheshire grin, she said, "Second of all I'm a black belt in Karate. I also hold degrees in Tae Kwan Do and Ju Jitsu."

"Which means you can't be harmed?"

"No. It doesn't mean that. But whoever tries isn't going to get away unscathed." She took a sip of her own wine. "That is if he gets away at all."

Victor grinned. As his eyes roamed over her gorgeous face he almost smacked his lips. He looked like a man who liked a challenge.

The waiter was pouring more wine when Victor's eyes darted over her shoulder. He had spotted someone. A minute later Jonathan approached. "Hello, Victor," he said. Nodding to Leah he said, "How are you? Please give my regards to David when you see him." Turning back to the Russian he said, "I was told you lunch here."

Victor nodded. "What more can I do for New York's finest? I thought I had answered all of your questions."

Jonathan said, "I have a few more for you since we spoke last."

"Could it wait till after lunch? Or perhaps we could talk at the bar?" he said, motioning toward the nearby bar.

Jonathan said, "Yes, that would be OK."

Dabbing at his lips with the white linen, Victor stood and gave an almost formal half bow to Leah. He said, "Would you be so kind as to excuse me for a moment, my dear?"

Leah, forking some poached salmon, simply nodded.

When Victor returned to the table Jonathan trailed him. He said, "Thank you, sir, for your time." Turning to Leah he said, "Would you and David be able to have dinner with my mother and I this evening?"

Victor carefully watched their faces as Leah said, "Yes, of course. Pick me up."

As lunch concluded, Victor motioned the waiter over. "Please have my car brought out front."

"Yes, sir."

Leah stood. "Would you mind if I left now? I have some shopping to do nearby."

"My limo is at your disposal."

"That's very kind but I need the exercise." She smiled. "Ciao."

"Ciao," he said, his eyes lingering on her as she strode out.

David was looking spry as he bounded out of the motel in his exercise clothes and hailed a cab to take him to the gym. Lou was at the front desk. He didn't appear friendly. David said, "How are you today, Lou?"

The little gym owner didn't make eye contact. David said, "Something wrong?"

Lou scratched his bald head. "Well, I hope you take it the right way, sir, but I think you've scared all my customers off."

"How so?"

"You beat the crap out of most of them."

David had to hold back a grin. "Oh, I see. Well, I'm sorry about that. I guess I'll be going then. I wasn't going to be around much longer anyway. I have my niece's funeral tomorrow and then I will be leaving. I'd like to thank you for your hospitality," he said, quickly adding, "thus far."

Having received a note from Leah that night that she would not be able to join him for dinner, he took a cab to the La Bernardin Restaurant at the Ritz Carlton at Central Park. He spotted Brenda and Jonathan immediately. They were sitting at a table that overlooked the Park.

As soon as he sat down he realized that Jonathan was going to be the spokesman for the decimated branch of the McAllister family. Jonathan asked, "Where's Leah?"

"She's made her excuses."

Jonathan's eyes caught David's. "Oh, I hope she's well."

"Yes, she's fine."

Jonathan said, "I just think she is not using good discretion in choosing her company these days."

"Why do you say that?"

"She was lunching with Victor this afternoon. I had to see him about Alicia's case."

Brenda stirred her martini. "That's unfortunate."

David said, "You might consider that our dear Leah is up to something. And I mean that in the best way. I mean something good. I believe she is trying to get information out of that wily Russian."

They lapsed silent while the hovering waiter waited stepped in to take their order. They were sipping drinks before anyone spoke. Jonathan said, "I was wondering if you had any thought on the eulogy for Alicia tomorrow."

David's face dropped. Then he looked up. "Yes, I have some ideas. No doubt I will not be able to do that fine young lady justice, but I'll try." His eyes moistening David added, "I want you to know I couldn't have loved that child more if she were my own."

Jonathan said, "Thanks, Uncle, I'm sure Dad would have appreciated that."

The words seemed to move Brenda. She squirmed in her chair, a comment on the tip of her tongue.

Before she could speak, David said, "I want to tell you that I am taking some steps to re-arrange my assets and I have included you folks in it." Brenda leaned forward as if she was about to speak but David kept talking. "I also want you to know that it has nothing to do with any feelings of guilt about my brother. While it's true that I do have remorse about my brother, my conscience is clear that I had nothing to with his demise in the sense of not helping him. I'm afraid that he lost sight of the most important thing in life and that is the importance, or rather the real place for wealth in our lives."

Brenda looked stunned. Jonathan said nothing.

David gazed at both of them. "I've had an epiphany in my life. I've come to realize that wealth doesn't really bring happiness. I know that sounds corny and cliché but I have really come to believe it. I studied all the great thinkers of our time to see what they thought and the one who came closest to how I feel is Andrew Carnegie."

"The rich, Andrew Carnegie?" Jonathan asked.

"That's the one," he said. "Carnegie said, 'Surplus wealth is a sacred trust which its possessor is bound to administer in his behalf for the good of the community.'"

"Pretty profound, Uncle."

"Well," David said tightening his lips, "for me it is going to be words to live by."

They all went back to quietly eating until Jonathan asked, "What are your plans after you leave New York?"

David wiped his lips, took a sip of wine and said, "After a stop in Chicago, I'm going to fly to Switzerland to join Albert there."

"Some spring skiing?"

"Yes, and also some meditation. No place like Switzerland to meditate. It's so quiet and peaceful."

Brenda said, "After all this I believe we could all use some quiet, peaceful time. For me the worst thing in the world is to survive a child and yet that is what I am going to have to live out the rest of my days with."

David looked at her thoughtfully. "You are absolutely right, Brenda. I, myself, feel the same way." He stopped to sip his drink. Then he raised his glass. "May I propose a toast to my dear niece." They all raised their glasses and clinked them one to the other. David said, "May she sleep with the angels."

Brenda let out a sob and David reached over and touched her arm. "I can make the two of you a sincere promise."

Jonathan cocked his head.

David said, "I will not rest until her murderer is brought to justice. I mean that literally. I will devote my life, if necessary, to find her killer."

Jonathan, his eyes wet said, "I'm with you, Uncle. I'm with you."

Chapter Seven

The organ pumped air into its pipes and the wailing music lifted to a crescendo and the haunting melody of the *Ave Maria* lingered a moment and then reverberated through the church. David dabbed at his eyes with a handkerchief. Now the sweet voices of the chorus themselves lifted the notes of the Ave to the heavens. Sobs filled the pew behind him. He knew Jonathan and Brenda were there.

It was cold and windy at the cemetery. David stood apart from the cluster of mourners, dressed in a long black coat belted at the waist, his hair whipping about in the breeze. His thoughts were of Alicia. It was a perfectly fitting day for a funeral but David thought, not the kind of day that would brighten the day of a free spirit like his dear Alicia.

As he got into the limousine for the drive to the reception, David thought, *I know this is no time for thoughts of revenge but God help me I can think of nothing else. I must remember not to dishonor dear Alicia in my obsession to see justice. I mustn't necessarily be sure that it is I personally who sees justice done, only that justice, indeed, is done.*

The mood at the family gathering afterwards, like all such social occasions was a bit less despondent. Although, not much. Alicia had been young and vivacious and her loss was very hard on her friends and family.

He was standing alone in a corner, nursing a martini, when Jonathan approached him, drink in hand. "Hello, Uncle. A sad day."

David said, "For all of us."

Jonathan, stifling a sob raised his glass and murmured, "To Alicia." They clinked glasses and took a sip. Waiters were wandering around the room with oeurvrs d'euves, but few had any appetite.

David asked, "Any leads in the case?"

"I'm afraid not. Whoever did it was expert in cleaning up the crime scene. There were no fibers, no blood splatter, no fingerprints, nothing."

"How about our friend Mr. Luchensko?"

"I've got him under surveillance twenty four seven and I will until we get a break or the Department pulls it off him. I have to admit, Uncle, although I'm determined to find the killer it is looking bad."

David thought a moment and said, "Don't feel that way, Jonathan, if nothing else, by keeping the man covered he is unlikely to do in some other poor young thing."

Jonathan took a sip, thinking. "I guess you're right. I want him bad but you know something?"

David waited.

"I think revenge isn't all it's cracked up to be. It'll never bring my sister back. Mother and I will miss her as long as we live."

"I know, Jonathan," he said, clamping a reassuring hand on the young man's shoulder. "While we shouldn't lust for revenge we should make sure that justice is done. Not only for our dear Alicia, but for any other victims of this…this SOB."

They lapsed silent for a while the reception buzzed around them. Then David asked, "What is the latest intelligence on this Luchensko fellow?"

Jonathan thought for a moment. "Well, we at first thought he was simply a part of the new Russian Mafia which has sprung up since the fall of the Soviet Union."

David raised a brow. "And…?"

"As it turns out, it might go deeper than simple racketeering."

"How so?"

"Well, there is a link, albeit tenuous, that this man is making money by helping terrorists."

David cocked his head. "How so, Jonathan?"

"He's supposed to be gun running. He has a segue through Mexico to get weapons out. From what I heard it's real sophisticated stuff too. No lousy AK's, and rocket propelled grenades, but SAMS, Stinger missiles and more."

"Wow," David said, snatching a fresh drink from a passing waiter.

Jonathan went on. "He's also helping them in other ways."

"Such as?"

Jonathan threw a furtive glance over his shoulder. "Uncle, a lot of this stuff is classified. I myself only know about it in a general way. I understand that the Department of Defense is also on his case."

"Well, that's good. Betters the chances of getting him."

"You might think so."

David waited.

Jonathan said, "Sometimes, the more fingers in the pudding the tougher it is. Then you get into inter agency squabbling. You know how it is. Everyone wants to get credit for the collar."

"Yes. I do know what you mean."

David leaned closer to his nephew. "Listen, Jonathan, I promise not to meddle in the investigation, but you know what I said the other day about getting this guy is not an idle threat."

"Yes, Uncle, I know."

"Well, could you tell me whatever else you know about this Mexico channel for arms?"

Jonathan drew his eyes away from his uncle. He seemed to be gazing over his shoulder. "I uh…."

David stopped him. "OK. I understand. I'm asking you to compromise your principles."

Jonathan hesitated. "Well, I …" He locked eyes with David and said, "Oh the hell. I couldn't give it to a more discreet person. Here's what I know."

David set his drink down and with a glance made sure there was nobody in earshot.

Jonathan said, "All I know is that there is a connection on the island of Cozumel. Something about them getting the arms out to Cuba on fishing boats. As you know, anything old Fidel can do to hurt America he'll gladly do. The Coast Guard or the State Department are aware but there's an awful lot of ocean down there to search."

"Thanks, Jonathan, I know it was tough for you to…"

Just then Brenda joined them. "Hello, David."

"Hello, Brenda. Jonathan and I were just saying how it is a sad day for all of us."

"Indeed. Our lives will never be the same."

"Agreed."

Brenda said, "Is Leah here?"

"She wasn't feeling well, she has asked me to convey her condolences. The bright yellow arrangement on the left of the coffin was from her."

Brenda said, "Oh, how thoughtful. Yes, I thought those flowers were particularly beautiful. Alicia loved yellow. Did Leah know that?"

"She must have," David said, his tone non-committal.

Leah touched up her lipstick before alighting from the limo. She was meeting Victor at Club 24. The two were drinking and seemed to be enjoying the date when Victor, in a most discreet way, asked, "How well do you know this fellow, David McAllister?"

Leah raised her martini glass to her lips and with a wry smile replied, "Jealous already? We hardly know each other."

Victor flashed her an equally crooked smile and answered, "I'm not jealous, darling. I'm a careful man. I do not need complications from other men in my, uhhh... affairs."

Leah cocked a brow. "Affair? Is that what we're having. I thought we were just having drinks in a friendly atmosphere. I never promised anything remotely like an affair."

Victor grinned. "Where else do relationships between men and women lead?"

"Maybe they lead to friendly drinks only. As for my relationship with David, not only is that personal but it would be irrelevant. I owe no man anything. My relationships can be as open as the sky."

Victor smiled broadly now. "Ah, a woman after my own heart. An affair without entanglements." He sipped his drink, and said, "But, what if, my dear, I do want an entanglement?"

"That's your problem."

Victor again smiled broadly.

Leah, looking coquettish also grinned. "I have a feeling, my dear Victor that you see that as a challenge. You don't really want to have a woman fall in love with you, but…you don't like the idea that she might not fall in love with you. I think you are used to having things your own way." She grinned again. "N'est ce pa?"

"Touché," he said raising his glass in a toast. "But we shall see."

Leah said, "Maybe. Mayyyybe," stretching out the last word and winking at him.

After another sip of her martini Leah cooed, "I thought you promised me a good time? Doesn't that include dancing?"

Victor stood up. "But of course, my dear." He offered his arm in an exaggerated chivalrous manner.

As they got into her limo, she said, "I'm leaving for London tomorrow so if you are enjoying my company I'd make a night of it."

Victor said, "You are quite right. I know a couple of trendy night spots in Tribeca and Soho you might like." With that he gave the driver an address.

After a couple more nightspots where they listened to jazz, saw a couple of belly dancers and drank Greek ouzo, they were finally back at Leah's hotel in the wee hours of the morning. Leah was in a good mood. A bit tipsy, she was singing from a Broadway musical of the 40s. "When a Broadway baby says good night……………. How does it go?"

Victor liked her lilting voice and finished off her lyric, "It's early in the morning."

It was almost four when Victor accompanied her to her hotel door. He gazed into her eyes, but found nothing serious. "So when are you leaving town?"

"In the afternoon."

"Could we have breakfast?"

"I'm afraid not. I have things to do in the morning. Besides, I'm pretty well looped. I'm going to sleep in."

He leaned toward her and sought her lips, managing only to brush them and being presented only with her soft cheek. He took advantage and did kiss it. Then his lips slid down to her neck where he again kissed her as she pulled away. "Thank you for a wonderful evening, Victor. I'll look you up when I get back in town."

The door was closed before Victor could say more. He raised his hand to knock on the door, but seemed to change his mind and with a shrug headed for the elevator.

In her room Leah lifted the phone. "Hello, this is Leah Hammond in the Executive Suite. Could you please make arrangements for me to fly to Cancun, Mexico in the morning? And the very next and the very best connection to the island of Cozumel." She listened for a moment and then repeated, "Yes, Cozumel. I believe that is spelled C O Z U M E L. And thank you very much. I've enjoyed your hotel's service very much this trip."

Chapter Eight

Jonathan was hard at work at his desk in the Detective Bureau when he was distracted by the staccato click clack of high heels on the marble floor of the Precinct House. He looked up to see a smiling Leah approaching him. She was wearing sunglasses but he was sure it was her.

She stopped at his desk and extended her hand. "Hello, Jonathan, I'm so sorry I couldn't make the funeral but I had this awful stomach flu. It really laid me out. David told me that it was a very touching affair. I know he was feeling the pain in the depths of him. He so loved Alicia."

Jonathan took her hand and said, " That's all right, Leah. I'm sorry to hear that you're not well. I hope you're feeling better."

"Yes, but my eyes are still so puffy I dare show them in public. Listen, Jonathan, do you have time for a cup of coffee? I'm on my way to the airport and I have a limo that will take me there afterwards."

Jonathan smiled. He closed the folder before him and returned it to a file. "Let's go," he said, taking her by the arm.

They found that the coffee shop downstairs wasn't very crowded since it was now mid morning. Everyone in the place knew Jonathan and he was able to get an almost quiet table in the corner.

Before the coffee was served she reached across the table and took his hands. "I know you've seen me with Victor Luchensko and you were probably wondering what I was up to. I want to tell you."

Jonathan's eyes narrowed. "I felt it was your own business."

"Well, David and I both know that Victor is Alicia's killer. David knows what I'm up to and what I am up to is to learn as much as I can about our elusive Mr. Luchensko."

"He's a dangerous man, Leah, I'm surprised David is letting you get involved."

Her pretty mouth twisted into a wry smile. She said, "If you knew me better you would understand that I'm a pretty independent person. All David can do is to tell me to be careful."

The coffee came and as both stirred in sugar and cream, Leah said, "My purpose in talking to you is two fold. First I wanted to tell you what I am doing with Luchensko and," her voice lowered now, "I was hoping that you could give me anything you know that might help me nail him. Because with the little time I've spent with him I am enough of a detective to know that he is involved in some nefarious projects. I also know that I'm not going to get anything more, or let me say anything at all, about Alicia's murder. He's too clever to let anyone know anything about that. He knows the consequences and although he loves women, he's too shrewd to put himself in danger for any woman. My thinking is that if we can't put him away for Alicia's murder we can put him away for something else."

Jonathan sipped some coffee and gazed at her. " I'm glad you're thinking that way because David seems to feel that he somehow has to off our dear Mr. Luchensko himself. I like the idea of putting him away too."

Leah again took his hand. "Jonathan, you have to understand something else. I would never, ever betray any confidence or any information you gave me. In a way telling David is like telling me. Neither of us would ever betray you."

"I hope you are not asking me to tell you what I know about him."

"Yes, Jonathan, that's exactly what I'm asking you. I am as committed as David and I won't rest until that Russian mobster is in jail with the rest of the animals."

Jonathan sipped more coffee. He looked at Leah. "Has David told you anything?"

"Yes. I'm being honest. He told me about the Mexico connection. He wouldn't have if he didn't trust me to the fullest."

Jonathan sighed. "He shouldn't have done that."

"But he did. And again, it's because he trusts me. You trust him, don't you?"

"Of course."

"Then you can trust me too. Now please tell me what you may know."

"There's nothing beyond what I told David. You say he told you."

"Yes. He is delivering sophisticated arms from Cozumel via Cuba and then somehow to Iraq."

Jonathan ran his hand nervously though his hair. "Whewww,' he said, "he did tell you."

"Yes. If you can tell me more I will be able to find out more."

Jonathan said, "I'm surprised David would let you do such dangerous stuff."

"Well he has. And the more you tell me maybe the less dangerous it will be."

"I assume nothing can change your mind and you are going to follow this Mexican connection no matter what."

"Yes."

He thought for a moment. "Well, you've put me in a spot, Leah. If I tell you, you will no doubt get into danger. If I don't you may get into even more."

"So you haven't told David everything?"

"No. I didn't want him going off into more danger. Now you have given me a dilemma that amounts to the same thing."

"I'm sorry, Jonathan, but as I said, I am as determined as David." She leaned forward and clasped his hand. "I don't have any more time. Are you going to tell me anything beyond Cozumel and the Cuba connection?"

Jonathan chewed his lip. Leah looked like she was about to get up when he said, "The fisherman in Cozumel is named Hector."

"Anything else?"

"No."

"A Mexican fisherman named Hector. That should be duck soup."

Jonathan grinned. "I'm not done."

She said, "Well?"

"I know that they go from Cozumel to Cuba to the UK. That's what makes it hard. The Cuban connection. We don't have much intelligence on it. But we have some Intel that suggests the stuff is going to a gang of Pakistanis in Manchester, England. You know where that is."

"Of course. And I know there is a large Pakistani population there."

Jonathan tapped his fingers nervously on the table. "I hope I haven't done something I'm going to regret. I didn't tell David everything because I wanted to dissuade him from going too far with this dangerous guy. Will David get involved along with you?"

"No. I need to work my womanly wiles alone. Besides, David respects my independent nature. That's why we get along so well. We don't get in each other's way. We're true to each other with no reservations but we operate independent of each other. I know it's unique, but that's the way we like it."

Jonathan's gaze was taking on more of a stare and Leah decided she had to go. "My flight is waiting, Jonathan. Thank you for your confidence in me. I promise you that you will never regret it."

She leaned down, pecked him on the cheek and was out the door. He saw her board a black Lincoln limo and watched it melt into the traffic flow of 52nd Street.

The twin engine Otter dipped its port wing and Leah could see the tiny island of Cozumel in the distance. The Otter was a small propeller aircraft that carried nineteen passengers on the short hop over from Cancun, Mexico. Below, a passenger ship made its way toward the island's only port.

The aircraft made a sickening lurch to starboard and began its descent to the island. The landing was bumpy; the wheels screeched and the props went into a roaring reverse thrust.

Leah grabbed a cab, which whisked her along the island's only road along the coast to the Melia International Hotel. It was a balmy day, and she gazed out the cab window at the sugar white beaches and jungle vegetation of the island. The ocean was an impossible aqua color with white foamed caps, which came ashore in an endless procession. From her travels, she knew the island was typical of these climes.

The hotel entranceway was lined with coconut palms. The afternoon trade winds rustled the fronds and all was serene. She wished her mission could enable her to enjoy this piece of paradise but she knew that wasn't the case. She knew that she was about to go into harm's way.

Chapter Nine

After unpacking and getting into more casual beachwear, a kind of sarong type dress, Leah slipped on her Foster Grants and headed for the ocean-side bar. She locked her room door and headed for the elevator. On her way she met a young couple coming up the hallway dressed in scuba gear and still wet, obviously coming in from a diving excursion. In a friendly way, she asked, "How's the diving?"

"Great," they said in unison as the guy swiped his card in his hotel room door. The girl, in a bikini, her skin now pimpled by the hotel air conditioning, was shivering. "I've dived everywhere. This water is the clearest I've ever seen. Brrr," she said, her teeth chattering as she dashed into the room.

"Do you dive?" the man asked standing in the doorway.

"Yes, but I haven't for a while. I may need a refresher lesson."

He held out his hand. "I'm Mark, and Bonnie and I would be glad to give you a lesson if you want to go out with us tomorrow."

"Why thanks," Leah said, "I'll look you guys up at breakfast in the morning."

"Good. See you then."

She knew that divers formed a kind of tight fraternity wherever they dived and one could always easily make friends.

At the bar, it was the cocktail hour but still not busy yet. The shimmering expanse of aqua Caribbean waters was darkening and the night sounds of insects chirping and whirring took over.

She planted herself on a bar stool at the far end and ordered something fruity. As she sipped she people watched. Cozumel was a magnet for all kinds of sun worshiping tourists but mostly for divers. This stretch of coast had the clearest waters in the Caribbean and it was purported that one could see forty feet while underwater just as if he was on the surface.

Several men gave her the eye but she ignored them and focused on the bartender, a tall slim Mexican with a thin black mustache. His name was Paolo. After some friendly banter and introductions, Leah said, "I know this may be a long shot, but do you know a fisherman in the village named Hector Morales?"

The bartender grinned, thinking she was making a pass, a suggestion she didn't want to dissuade him from. "No, but I have a friend, he works for Room Service, his brother is a fisherman in the village. I could ask him."

"Would you?" Leah asked sweetly. Then she added, "I may turn in early, I'm tired form a day of traveling. What's your friend's name?"

The bartender seemed disappointed but said, "He is Carlos Montana."

"Thanks," she said, and slid off the bar stool, leaving him a generous tip. "I'll see you tomorrow."

The bartender smiled broadly. "I will be here, Senorita Leah."

The drinks had stimulated her appetite so back in her room she ordered a seafood platter and a Mexican beer for dinner. She asked Room Service for a particular waiter, one Carlos Montana.

When the meal arrived, she noticed the waiter's name tag, Carlos Montana. She said, to him, "Did your friend Paolo tell you I asked to see you?"

"No, Senorita," he said with a little tilt of his head. "I haven't seen Paolo today. I came into work late."

She lowered her thick lashes in the alluring way she did when she wanted to interest men. Carlo was no exception. He paid attention to her. She said, "I have a friend back home who knows one Hector Morales, he is a fisherman, and my friend asked me to say hello and give him his new address in New York. Paolo says you might know him."

"Well, I know a Hector, who is a fisherman. I have done some part time work on his boat when things are slow. That's how I know him. But, I'm not sure if his last name is Morales."

"Oh," said Leah, disappointed. "I..."

The waiter said, "All I know is that he has a Cuban wife. She is uh, uh how do you say uh... elegant, and very pretty I might add."

Leah, cocking a brow, perked up, saying, "You seem like Hector doesn't deserve a pretty wife."

Carlos said, "I don't mean that, Senorita. I guess what I mean is that Hector is a very common man. A poor Mexican fisherman. His wife, Manuella, is pretty and...how do you say it. Ahh...nice manners, speaks well."

"You mean sophisticated?"

"Si, si, Senorita. That's what I mean."

Leah fished out his hefty tip from her purse and while handing it to him asked, "What boat is his?"

Carlos hesitated. "Uhh....let me see. Uh, she is *Manuella*."

Leah nodded. "Thanks very much, Carlos. Have a nice night."

"Si, Senorita. Say hello to Hector for me."

As Leah picked at her seafood and sipped her beer she made some phone calls. First she called the Playa del Sol Hotel. "Hello, Executive Reservations? My name is Mrs. Leah Luchensko, my husband Victor Luchensko has asked me to book him his usual suite for next week."

"Spell the name please, Senora."

She spelled it and waited. A few minutes later he said, "I'm sorry, Senora, we have no record of a person with this name as staying at our hotel."

"Thank you. My mistake."

Next was the Playa del Mar, the Hotel Aguilar the Costa Brava, the Fuenta Americana and the Cozumel Palace. After covering most of the major hotels on the island she got lucky at the Casa Del Mar. "Si, Senora, Senor Luchensko uses our Presidential Suite whenever he is here. When do you say he is coming?"

"I want to double check with him and I will call you back."

"Very well, Senora."

Leah was pleased with her progress so far and she ate more heartily. *So, our Victor does come here. There is a fisherman named Hector. And lo and behold he has a Cuban wife, whose sophistication seems oddly incongruent for a humble Mexican fisherman. How very convenient.*

Chapter Ten

Leah was having breakfast on the patio when Mark and Bonnie stopped by her table. Mark said, "You still up for diving today?"

"I sure am. Do you guys have a boat?"

"We usually go out with a group of six on their boat. But they're not around today so we are going to rent our own. Do you have your gear ready?"

"Yes. I rented it this morning. And please while you have breakfast let me rent us a boat. It's the least I can do."

They exchanged a pleased glance and nodded. "Okay."

"Great. See you out front in about an hour?"

"We'll be there."

Leah was hoping to convince the couple to dive near the fishing boat anchorage. And she was sorely in need of a refresher lesson in diving too.

A few hours later, on the boat, Mark and Bonnie gave her the refresher she needed. They went over all the safety precautions, and use of the guage's and the signals to give each other underwater including the dreaded hand across the throat meaning "I'm out of air. Need to go up."

Feeling more confident Leah stuck the mouthpiece in and dropped backward off the gunwale of the boat. Soon she was finning around underwater like a professional. When they were ready to go out she asked, "Could you do one more thing for me? I want to make one dive over near those fishing boats."

"Why?" Mark said, "it's a lot more interesting out on the reef. All kinds of fish and stuff."

"I know but I'm doing some research work on marine growth and I want to take a closer look at the bottoms of a couple of those boats."

Mark said, "Okay, Babe. It's your boat. But then it's out to the reef. Okay?"

"Right."

They motored over to the fishing boat anchorage. In a cursory sweep Leah spotted *Manuella*. She was a typical fishing boat covered with nets and gear and badly in need of paint. All three geared up and got in the water. While Bonnie and Mark occupied themselves nearer the seaside, Leah swam over to the boats.

She emerged from the water on the seaward side, out of sight of anyone on shore or Bonnie and Mark. Carefully she hauled herself up and slithered over the gunwale. Keeping low, she padded over to the hatch and went down stairs. There was a cheap lock on the door. She reached into her hair, withdrew a long thin pin like device and quickly picked the lock.

She searched the cabin thoroughly but found nothing. She was about to leave when something occurred to her. The life jacket locker. Down here in the cabin was an odd place to have it if someone went overboard. She decided to go through the life jacket locker once more. She pulled out the life jackets and this time and ran her hands over the bulkhead walls. Then she rapped each section. One section sounded hollow. She ran her fingernails along the edges and when she found an opening wide enough to accommodate her nails she pulled and a piece of panel came off. Inside was a strongbox. She pulled it out. It was locked so she went to work with her lock pick.

When she got it open she found some boat papers but under them were several Western Union messages. They originated in New York and were signed with a simple L. Hmmm, Luchensko, *maybe?* The messages didn't make much sense and she was about to leave when she decided to photograph them. Then, since she would have to wait for the photos to be developed she jotted them down on a slip of paper. She fished her tiny camera from her waterproof belly pack and photographed them. Then she put everything, including the copied messages, away.

Back on deck she was about to slip over the side when she heard her name being called. It was Mark and Bonnie. They had moved the boat closer to the *Manuella* and evidently were concerned when they couldn't find her. Not wanting them to see her on the boat she crawled over to the port side and near the boat, on a spot blocked by the cabin, she crawled over the side and slipped quietly into the water. She swam away from *Manuella* underwater and popped up a dozen yards seaward. She raised her arm and called, "Hey, guys, I'm over here."

They swam over. Mark said, "You shouldn't go so far from us. Like I told you one of the first rules of diving is stay with or near someone."

Leah said, "I'm sorry, guys. I got carried away. Listen, I probably overdid it anyway, my first day back in the water. I'm really tired. I'm going to go ashore--it's only a hundred yards--and grab a cab back to the hotel. You guys are welcome to use the boat all day."

Bonnie said, "Are you sure? If you're tired are you sure you can make it ashore?"

Leah said, "Oh yeah. I've got enough left in me for that."

Mark said, "Okay, but we're going to swim in with you to make sure you're safe."

With a reluctant nod Leah agreed and they all swam ashore. Leah said, "Thanks a lot, guys. I had enough fun for today. I'll see you back at the hotel."

They went back in the water and Leah headed for the main street of the village, San Pedro. She caught a cab and went back to the hotel.

In her room she got into comfortable clothes and lay on the bed perusing the copied Western Union messages. Since they made no sense as written she tried a couple of combinations of methods, such as skipping every other word. That didn't come up with anything sensible. So she tried various combinations such as working backward and skipping every two words. But it was boring and tiring work and worn out by the diving, she fell asleep.

She awoke refreshed and ordered coffee and pecan rolls from Room Service and went back to work. When she answered the knock at the door it was Room Service and the waiter was Carlo.

"Oh, hello, Carlo," she said admitting him.

He gave her a pleasant smile and said, "Have you been able to find Hector?"

"No, but I will before I leave. Uh, tell me, Carlo. Do you have any idea how Hector met Manuella. She is a Cuban. Not many Cubans are allowed to live abroad."

"Oh, she was a flight attendant for Air Cuba. They fly into Cancun."

"And they got married and she was allowed to live here?"

Carlo shrugged. "Si. I guess so, Senora. I don't really know. I just know most of us know that she is a foreigner. Not many on Cozumel marry foreigners."

"I can see that." She tipped him generously and with a smile he left.

Leah lazily sipped her coffee and munched her rolls out on her balcony but her mind was busy. *Hmm. A Cuban for a wife on an island where the poor Mexicans are lucky to meet and marry someone above their class. A very convenient connection for someone involved in the gun running trade.*

She went back to trying to decode the messages as she was convinced they were coded.

By early evening her bed was covered with crumpled pieces of paper, as every combination of code she tried proved wrong. Finally she put in a call to Albert in England. He was happy to hear from her. When she told him where she was he said, "What? What are you doing there?"

"It's a rather long story, Albert. But I need your help."

"Yes?"

"Do you still have contact with that friend who worked for MI6?"

"Why yes. We still have dinner about once a month. Why?"

"I need a favor." She quickly gave him the messages and asked him to see if his friend could make sense of it. She knew it was a code but didn't have the expertise to figure it out. Albert promised to run the messages by his friend and call her back.

She was downstairs in the bar having a cocktail when the call came through. They patched it through to the bar phone. Albert said, "Where are you? It sounds noisy."

"I'm in the hotel bar."

"Oh dear," he said sounding worried.

"What is it, Albert?"

"I do hope you don't get yourself into any trouble. After all, David doesn't have friends on the police force in Mexico."

"Don't worry, Albert, I'm being as nice as the Queen down here. You wouldn't recognize me."

She could almost see Albert's wry grin over the phone. "Now tell me," she said, "any luck?"

"Yes, actually." He paused.

"Well tell me, Albert. I'm dying of suspense."

"I do hope this won't get you into any trouble."

"Well, tell me and then I'll know that too." She was getting impatient and quickly.

Albert cleared his throat. The message, decoded said, 'You are clear to land at point AZX at Point of Pines at 2100 hours on 6 June. Password is Viva Fidel.'

The other two messages were similar but with different dates, landing sites and passwords.

"Thanks so much, Albert. I'll be heading home soon. I'll see you then."

"Uh, is David coming home too?"

"I believe he is heading for Switzerland. I'll be there too after a brief stay in London."

"Very well. See you soon. And do be careful."

Chapter Eleven

The British Airway 777 made a sickening lurch to starboard as David gazed down at the Thames and the city beyond. As usual British Airways was right on time.

By the time the big jet landed it was 11:00 a.m. local time. He just had time to run a few errands in London before returning to Heathrow Airport for the flight to Geneva. He had his luggage transferred to the Swiss Air flight before he left the airport.

The weather report on the airport monitors showed lots of snow in the major ski areas of Switzerland. His chalet was near the town of Zermatt and Switzerland's famed Matterhorn, a picturesque mountain that straddled the Swiss Italian border.

As they flew over Switzerland from the northwest at 30,000 feet David marveled at the rugged splendor of the Alps, an endless sea of rugged, almost jagged, snow covered peaks. The Alps are a geological array of rugged mountains formed by the collision of African and European tectonic plates. And it was one of the world's major playgrounds for winter sports enthusiasts. He recalled that the forecast promised bad weather for the weekend but he still had good weather for the rest of the week to get in some skiing.

By the time they crossed the big lake and lined up on the Geneva runway it was mid afternoon.

Albert spotted him amid a sea of bobbing heads as he entered the baggage area. The butler was smiling broadly when he met him at the baggage carousel. David gave him a big hearty hug and they were off to the chalet. It was a three-hour drive along the lake and then into the mountains. Albert filled him in on weather and local gossip before he asked about things in New York. He was saddened by the details of Alicia's funeral. He wiped away a tear and said, "That lovely lass. I hate the idea that we will never see her again."

"I know what you mean, old friend. I am having trouble coping myself."

It was almost dark when they pulled up to the chalet. It was typically Tyrolean, log walls with the A framed roof. It was two storied with ornately carved balustrades on both levels. Potted green plants hung everywhere. Inside there was a huge rock fireplace and a cathedral ceiling that soared to the uppermost ceiling. A sleeping loft on the second floor, the only break in space. The kitchen was European with the center island and large black kettles and pots handing over it. The kitchen was full of baskets and bunches of fresh vegetables and small bowls of spices and herbs. The cook was busy with dinner. David greeted her, an older French woman who had worked for him for years. "Bonjour, Monsieur Davide," she crooned, as she approached him open armed.

"Bonjour, Marie. What magic are you cooking up for us this evening?"

David had always kept life at the chalet very informal and he usually ate with Albert, Marie and whatever guests were around.

After a gourmet dinner of veal smothered in an exquisite sauce that was addictive, David and Albert chastised each other for reaching for seconds. Finally, patting their bellies, David crooned, "Marie, you are a national treasure."

She blushed and waved her hand at him, while loving the praise.

David and Albert had a brandy late that evening by the fire. Marie had already gone home. David said, "I again want to thank you, Albert, for all your help."

"That doesn't mean I agree with what you are doing. I know your motives are strong and valid, I...well, I guess I wish there was another way."

David finished his drink and patted Albert's knee. "Well I'm off to bed old chum".

David usually skied with the guests but there was no one with him when he took the cable car to the six thousand foot level. He stared up at the majesty of the Matterhorn, its peak veiled in a gauzy white cloud cover. As he adjusted his goggles for the run down to the village he heard the sunbathers and diners at the midway restaurant clapping. It was a column of Italian Alpine troops crossing one of the mountains glaciers resplendent in their feathered caps and in a long single file slowly moving across the glacier.

He poled over to the edge of the ski trail and gazed down at the snow prairies. There were no trees to contend with on the trail for at least three thousand feet. He took a big breath of the fresh mountain air, adjusted his goggles once more and pushed off.

It was a delightful sail down the white snowfields. He reveled in the joy of it making huge, sweeping turns as the tree line slowly grew darker and larger.

He rested at the point in the trail where the tree line started. He would have to be more careful the rest of the way down to the village. After a couple of gulps of coffee from his thermos in his belly pack he also had a bite of Toblerone chocolate for energy and again pushed off.

He was back at the chalet by mid afternoon, ready for a nap and another one of Marie's extravagant meals.

When she was clearing his dishes away, Marie, with an unusual look of concern on her face told David, "You must be *tres careful, demain Monsieur,* everyone in the village is concerned about avalanches."

"You know everyone in the village is superstitious about the mountain, Marie. Most times it is just rumor."

"But the government, monsieur, they have put out the signs too. You must be careful. The mountain, Matterhorn ees so beautiful but every year that beautiful mountain kills some unsuspecting people."

David gave her his best happy go lucky smile and then went on to compliment her about dinner.

In the morning he again set out for the slopes. Marie was right. There were signs out and people were talking about it. But without hesitation he boarded the cable car and as usual got off at the six thousand foot level. High above, the Matterhorn's peak was lost in a thick and darkening cloud. The valley was covered in deep shadow and David hunched his shoulders against the shiver of portent that went up his spine.

The news reached the chalet by evening. There had been avalanches. The government was looking for volunteers. They knew that at least six people were killed and over forty missing. Albert did his best to calm Marie down as she was near panic.

The usual time period for the search and rescue portion of a search was two days to find living avalanche victims but after that it became a recovery mission. That's after they had tried everything including sound devices, dogs and aerial photography.

The newspaper had reported some spectators hearing a loud blast before the big snow slide but nobody could confirm it. Because of that report and also the fact that the avalanche did not happen in an area where avalanches typically occurred, there was sure to be further investigation.

Albert got the final word four days later that David McAllister, his long time employer and dear friend was considered dead. The police advised him that in such cases where no body can be found, at least still spring and at that altitude, probably never, the case was considered closed. There had been instances of avalanche victims showing up dazed and battered a week later, but that was the stuff of miracles. For all practical purposes, David was dead and Albert prepared a memorial service for him. He began dispatching telegrams to the family in New York and other places where David had friends.

Leah sent him a message, which was garbled and confused, no doubt due to her grief.

Jonathan called from New York. "When do you plan the memorial, Albert?"

"This next weekend. I'm hoping you can come."

"Yes. Mother and I will be there. I feel terrible. Uncle David was the closest thing I've had to a father or brother since Dad died."

"I know, Jonathan. I know. We are all going to miss him terribly."

Brenda got on the line. "Albert, did you know that David had seen that we got a huge inheritance even before he died? I just got the letter from the bank recently."

"Yes. I knew. While he didn't feel responsible for his brother's death he had decided on a different life's path and so gave away much of his money. He wanted to be sure you and David got a good share of it."

The line went silent. Albert said, "Brenda? Are you there?"

"Yes, Albert. I know it's too late now but I feel terrible for the thoughts I had about David. It's true none of his brother's fate was his fault. I was just bitter and not thinking straight. I'm so darn sorry I felt that way. Deep in my heart I knew he loved us all and especially Alicia. I feel like a worm."

"Well, at least now, Brenda," he said, "you know the truth and can feel good about David and his memory."

Jonathan got back on the line. "Albert, you know Uncle David was hard at work in trying to snare Alicia's killer?"

"Yes, I know. He was quite determined. In fact, between you and I he was convinced that if justice was not be found for Alicia that he himself would put an end to Mr. Victor Luchensko."

Jonathan said, "I was afraid of that. I didn't want to see him or any of us get into trouble and face jail in trying to get justice for Alicia. I too, knew he was determined."

"Indeed, sir."

"Albert, could you do me a favor."

"Anything, sir."

"If anything David found out turns up in his papers or anything that is held in probate for a while, will you let me know that evidence?"

"Yes, Jonathan. "I'm sure that's what David would have wanted."

"Thanks…"

Albert interrupted, "I certainly hope, Jonathan, that you yourself are careful about this matter. It is not worth the loss of your life to avenge Alicia. Your mother would then be alone and devastated, so please let things take their course. If necessary we can put private detectives on the trail. I want to keep you and your mother safe."

Jonathan sighed. The phone line crackled. Finally he said, "I know what you mean and in order to spare my mother more pain I'm more than inclined to take your advice. So please don't worry about it. But do send me whatever evidence turns up in Uncle David's papers. Thanks again and God bless. We'll see you this weekend."

"God speed, sir."

Chapter Twelve

The memorial reception for David was planned in a Zermatt chapel for the afternoon, but several friends and associates had already gathered at the chalet. Everyone wore the mask of grief since such a promising young person had died so tragically. The weather was cooperating; it was dark and gloomy.

Jonathan and Brenda had already arrived and were sipping a cocktail provided by a waiter staff that Albert hired. Albert had taken Jonathan aside to a quiet corner. The older man was pale and drawn. "My goodness," he said, shifting his feet, "this is the day for grief. I've just received some terrible news."

Jonathan cocked a brow and waited. Albert said, "Leah has been involved in a bad accident in England. She had been in England on an errand for David. It seems she was driving on a rain swept highway and was side swept by some bloke from the States who wasn't used to driving on the right side of the road."

"My God. How is she?"

"Not good I'm afraid. I made sure she was sent to a private hospital and they are not at all sure of her prospects. It will be touch and go."

"I'm so sorry, Albert. I hope that you will keep us advised. I mean even after we leave. A simple postcard or E mail will do."

"Of course, Jonathan. Now. There is something else I must talk to you about regarding Leah."

Intent now, Jonathan leveled his gaze at Albert.

Albert said, "Last week I received a courier package from Leah. It was from Mexico. Now mind you I had no idea what she was up to. That is until she called me prior to this and asked me to ask a friend at MI6 to decipher what was obviously code."

"What was the original document?"

"They are simple Western Union telegrams. The package contained some photographs. They contained photos of the original documents. Leah called that afternoon to explain more."

"Go on."

"Evidently she learned that our Victor Luchensko was involved with a terrorist group running guns to the UK via Cuba."

Jonathan's face betrayed him. Albert continued, "You, uh, know something about this?"

"I'm afraid so."

"Do you want to tell me or would you rather I go on?"

"Go on please," said Jonathan.

"Well, she has learned that Victor has a connection through a fisherman in Cozumel. Evidently they run their fishing boat into Cuba and either load or offload the weapons. Something in the coded messages suggests that this is sophisticated stuff like Stinger missiles."

Jonathan couldn't keep silent. "Damn. I told her about it but I never dreamed she would go so far with it."

"Oh, if you knew our Leah, you'd realized that's exactly what she would do. She has also been able to ascertain that Mr. Luchensko visits Cozumel regularly and knows the name of his hotel."

Jonathan sipped his drink. "Looks like she knows what he's up to but now we need solid proof in order to get our friends in the Bureau to raise their interest level."

"What can we do?"

"Well, first we need to get more solid information on Victor."

"Do you think your colleagues in the Federal government will only be interested if you can offer them more?"

"That's pretty much it."

Now Albert lapsed contemplative. Jonathan waited. "David has left me a considerable amount of money and I am not hesitant on spending some of it to help bring Alicia's murderer to justice."

"I appreciate how you feel, Albert, but David has left Mother and I a considerable amount too. Is money the issue though?"

"Well, as I see it, sir, it is a matter of resources. I'm afraid your New York Police Department and the FBI need more motivation if they are going to use some of their resources. To them it's just a routine murder. What I'm thinking is that we hire a private investigator. If he is right behind Luchensko on his next trip to Cozumel we can gather some more incriminating evidence which will help hang him."

"That's a good idea, Albert. I'm all for it. If I can go to the Feds with something solid like that buttressed by this other evidence we might be able to get the bastard as well as stop his terrorist friends."

"Evidently the key to this fisherman fellow in Cozumel is his Cuban wife. She is a flight attendant for Air Cuba."

Jonathan nodded. "Ah, a perfect cover for a spy. Most of the people in the Cuban embassy and those working for the national airlines are on Fidel's payroll."

"Hmm," Albert said, "That goes for visiting people in the cultural world, like musicians and singers. People like that."

"In the case of the airline people I'm sure it's a 'or else' type of job." He held his glass up for a passing waiter to re-fill. "Leah has provided us with a picture of her. Evidently she got it on the fellow's boat. The word in Cozumel is that this lady is much too sophisticated to be married to a fisherman like Hector."

"Probably a temporary set-up while Hector is in the gun running business to Cuba. I understand it is not easy to get into Cuba, although you tell me that most of the landing sites are obscure, like the Isle of Pines and places like that."

"True. Can you recommend a good PI in the States? Or would you rather be more distanced since you are a NYPD detective?"

"I'll let you pick one, Albert. You're right, it's not good I know the man. The more distance the better when it comes time to make our case. If we can hang a terrorist charge on Victor that's just as good as Murder One. They'll lock him up forever. Besides, unless someone rats him out we'll never get Murder One on him. He's too clever."

"Very good, sir. Then I'll see you at the service then." With that Albert was off to greet other mourners.

By early afternoon the chalet was becoming crowded but the place emptied out for the service. Albert had arranged for a fleet of limos to take the mourners to the service at the quaint little chapel in the village. It was David's church when he was in Zermatt and he often came here on odd days of the week.

As the mourners entered, air piped into the organ and *Ave Maria* burst forth and the music climbed to the steepled cathedral ceiling. All eyes sought out a large picture of David on the altar. It was festooned with flowers and messages of condolence from all over the world. The overflow covered the floor from wall to wall.

Brenda began to sob. Jonathan took her by the arm. The pastor's remarks were kept brief so that a few friends and colleagues could speak.

After a particularly moving talk by a colleague in the legal profession, Albert took the podium. People were still sobbing.

Albert scanned the room, cleared his voice and began to speak. "Weep no more, my friends. Your friend and colleague wouldn't want that." He paused and waited as people controlled themselves.

"Some of you are wondering why I, a butler and manservant, am up here to speak about my former employer David McAllister. And I will explain. In a moment. First let me say that it is said that only fools and Christians celebrate death. David was no fool. That's for sure, but knowing the man he was I'm certain that he is now in the heavenly embrace of the Father Almighty. I can be sure of this because I have observed the man from close quarters for years and I can tell you this. He never let a friend down. Nobody, truly in need and worthy, ever came to him and was rejected. He never betrayed a confidence. He never shirked from his responsibilities both as a barrister and as a man. He was always ready to cheer up those who were depressed. Always ready to give hope to those who felt hopeless. I'm not saying that David was a saint. He was human in every way. It came to him near the end of his life that he wanted to give his wealth away to others and to worthy causes. In his law career he had a special place in his heart for the hopeless and the helpless and the simply unfortunate. He would never tell anybody but David McAllister carried a caseload of more pro bono cases than any attorney in the Realm."

"True, in the beginning he was as ambitious as any young man on the rise and didn't have these values, but life taught them to him and he felt the need to help."

"So that brings me to why I am here. I'm here because David was more than my employer of many years but my friend. I've always felt a paternal instinct towards him but he wouldn't have it. He was more the one to care for others than the other way around."

"He was my dear friend and I'm sure that in this lifetime I will not be fortunate enough to have another friend the likes of him. With that I bid him good-bye and farewell and while the rest of us continue to toil on this earth I know he is looking down with his usual concern for all of us."

Despite Albert's prior admonition sobs again broke out and the organ played David's favorite hymn.

After the last organ note people began to file out. The clouds had been whisked away and bright sunshine flooded the valley. The air was crisp and clean and Albert sighed and murmured under his breath, "Rest in peace, old friend."

Chapter Thirteen

It was a cloudy day in Sussex. Thick gray clouds seemed to hang treetop low. The Rolls limousine pulled off the main highway onto a small gravel road. Its engine purring it moved down the country lane and turned off at a sign that read FERNWOOD HOSPITAL. Smaller signs advised that this was a private hospital and that there was no trespassing. The driver pulled up close to an electronic speaker and mentioned a password. A minute later a voice preceded by some static admitted them and the tall wrought iron gate swung open.

Albert alighted from the limo and stretched his legs. It had been a long ride from Heathrow. He gazed around. The hospital looked like it had been a mansion in another life. It was majestic, three stories high and made of round stone. It had several turrets and was covered with ivy, definitely a throwback to the Victorian era. The grounds were extensive all manicured green as far as the eye could see. The shrubbery and landscaping that hugged the place showed the care of professionals.

As he started for the front door he noticed several patients being wheeled around by white clad nurses with blue capes. The patients had blankets on their laps.

Inside he spoke to the receptionist. "Good morning. My name is Albert Farthington and I have an appointment to see Ms. Leah Hammond. It was authorized by her doctors."

The receptionist consulted her computer. Then she looked up at him. "Yes, Mr. Farthington. But please realize there is a time limit. Ms. Hammond has just had some initial surgery and her visitations are quite limited. So please limit your visit to one hour and please don't give the patient any type of food or candy before checking with us."

Albert nodded and was led by an orderly to Leah's room. They passed several empty rooms and Albert was certain that Leah's privacy and wishes were being observed. She was nowhere near any other patients. A minor celebrity, she didn't want to be pestered with any questions about herself or David.

She was sitting up in bed her face swathed in bandages. Nearby a nurse in a starched white uniform complete with cap hovered over and tinkered with some electronic monitoring devices that were hooked up to Leah. Albert muttered, softly, "Leah."

She looked his way. "Oh dear Albert. It's so good of you to come. Come here, let me give you a hug." Albert moved toward her with open arms. He said, "I don't want to hurt you. You look so...so frail."

"I can stand a hug." She opened her arms and they shared a rather tender, but awkward hug. She said, "I was heartbroken that I couldn't make David's memorial. As soon as I can walk I'm going to come to Switzerland to visit his memorial."

Albert lit up. "And you will of course stay with us at the chalet. That would be so wonderful. So, like..."

"Old times?"

"Yes. Yes that's true." Patting her hand he continued, "But there's plenty of time for that, my dear. Right now we have to make sure you are on the road to recovery. I understand from your doctors that it will be a long road indeed."

"I'm afraid that's so. And I'm going to need some facial surgery."

Albert said, "I'm sure it'll make you even more beautiful."

"Thanks, Albert. You really know how to cheer a girl up." The shared a conspiratorial grin and twinkle of the eye.

Lapsing serious Albert said, "Do you want to talk about what happened? What caused the accident?"

She paused, the eyes deep in the bandages blinking back tears. "I've been laying here thinking about that. I know I was depressed about David. I know I wasn't paying attention to the road. In fact I was daydreaming about meeting him in Switzerland for his birthday. But that's all I remember. The rest is a big blur."

Leah broke the awkward silence that followed by speaking to the nurse. She caught the nurse as she was leaving the room. "Miss Ford, is it possible that my guest and I could have some tea. It is almost tea time."

"I'll advise the culinary staff, Miss."

"Fine. And some of those wonderful cinnamon crumpets you serve."

"As you wish, Miss."

About ten minutes later, Albert and Leah were having a rather delightful tea under the circumstances. Leah said, "Do you have any feedback from Jonathan about our friend Mr. Luchensko and his gun running activities?"

Albert sipped some tea and set the cup down. "Well, believe it or not it is not as easy as it was prior 9/11 to deal with the Federal authorities on this subject. Now with the Department of Homeland Security running things, nobody wants to step on anybody else's toes so an investigation is harder to get going. And since all we have so far is some suspicion albeit backed by some evidence, Jonathan has not yet convinced anybody in authority that Mr. Luchensko should be investigated. Add to that the matter is really out of his jurisdiction seeing that the alleged crimes are being committed in Mexico, Cuba and the UK, I'm sure you can understand."

"I see," she said. "Then it is up to us to keep gathering information. I have a couple of good private investigators that I'll keep on his tail while I'm in the hospital. I want pictures of him talking to people like Hector and his wife and to the Arabs in Manchester in the UK who are sending the shipments on to the Middle East. We know about the Mexican Cuban connection but now we need to find out about how the weapons are trans-shipped from the UK to the war zone. With any luck we will not only nail Luchensko but will do the whole Western world a lot of good by plugging up a source of weapons."

Albert looked skeptical. "I do hope you will keep me, how do the Americans say it…in the loop?"

"Of course, Albert. As you can see we not only have to get the evidence on him but we have to set up a sting. Some way that he can fall into the hands of the Feds. It won't do us much good if we expose him to the Mexican or Cuban governments. You can see where that will go."

"Yes, nowhere. I see your point. We have to find a way to get him caught by those who have an interest in bringing him down. And you are right, that will not include the Mexicans or Cubans."

Albert seemed to be able to read her thoughts right through the bandages. He said, "I know you are going to be safely out of things for the time being, but I hope you are not planning anything very dangerous on this matter."

"Don't worry, Albert. I plan to get him, but I don't plan to get hurt in the process. It's obvious to me that we are not going to get him for Alicia's murder, and that the only way we are going to get him is on this gun running thing."

Albert gazed at her. "Revenge is not sweet if we lose you over it. Then it won't be sweet but only bitter. We don't need that, my dear. All we really need is that Mr. Victor Luchensko leave this mortal coil."

Leah sipped her tea. "If we were of another mind, Albert, we could simply hire the right person to bring swift justice to him."

Albert grinned. "A hit man?"

Leah smiled through the bandages. "I can see that you are not adverse to the idea and in a certain way I am too. But. And this is a big but. That is not our style but it would leave me with very little satisfaction."

Albert sighed and took another sip of tea. "Indeed. But it would be so much easier and safer."

Leah said, "You're just thinking of my safety, Albert. There's more to this than my safety. This monster has not only killed our Alicia but he's dispatched a whole batch of unsuspecting young girls. Girls who were drawn to his roguish character and good looks. Unfortunately some women are drawn to danger, like the fly to the web and then they are trapped and killed."

Albert nodded as Leah turned thoughtful. She said, "It's a failure of the female gender I'm afraid."

Looking confused, Albert asked, "What is that, dear?"

"Evidently for modern women, the love of a good man is not all that is necessary for fulfillment. There is also this need to challenge ourselves by co-horting with dangerous men. Women do it all the time. They shun the safe, square everyday guy for the gangster or the test pilot, or the police detective. They seem to be attracted by the adrenalin rush of danger, the idea of surviving the danger, the thrill of it all. It's as if life is not worth living unless we are challenging the fear. We are sky diving, mountain climbing, bungee jumping, running the rapids. You name something dangerous and women today are doing it."

Albert said, "You are right of course. But all that gives us old gentle types is what do the Italians call it?" he said rubbing his chest.

"Agita?" she quipped.

"Yes. Agita. Heartburn. And heartache."

The nurse appeared in the doorway and from the no nonsense look on her face, Albert knew his visit was over. He leaned over and hugged Leah, murmuring, "Get well soon, my dear. We are looking forward to getting you up to the chalet, where I will have Marie prepare you such wonderful dishes that you will quickly fatten up."

Chapter Fourteen

Albert waited at the window like an expectant father. There had been snow squalls in the Geneva area and he wondered if Leah's flight from London had been delayed. He had a limo at the airport waiting and he had expected her to arrive by now.

Marie had prepared Leah's favorite dinner of couscous and French pastries. The last of the medical equipment had been installed in the basement medical facilities, complete with operating room. He had assembled the best doctors on the continent for the work Leah needed. His plan was that Leah should have a relaxing lapse from hospital care for a couple of weeks before the serious surgery would begin. He knew that Leah might argue with him about the little vacation he had planned but he was prepared to fight her on it

He peered into the gray afternoon for the limo. He had left the window for a moment to answer some question of Marie's and when he returned the limo had already pulled up. Albert buttoned his topcoat and hurried out to greet Leah. "Ah, you're here. I was afraid you had been delayed."

Leah was looking better although a lot of her head was still swathed in bandages. "Just a little bumpy coming over, Albert. But I'm glad to be here."

Albert motioned for the driver to bring in the luggage while he escorted Leah into the spacious ground floor of the chalet. Marie came running from the kitchen wiping her hands on her apron. "Oh Madame, I am so happy to see you." She pronounced the "see" with a z sound. With the delicacy appropriate toward a recently infirm person Marie tenderly embraced Leah giving her soft hugs. Leah murmured, "Marie, all I could think about while I was eating the dreadful hospital cooking in England was, just wait, soon I will be eating Marie's inimitable cousine."

Marie glowed. "Oh, Madame. You are so kind. It is so good to have you home."

"Yes, home," Leah said, almost in a whisper. "Home."

Albert was beaming. He said, "I know what you mean about the cooking, Leah. Since I'm spending all of my time here instead of England, I've put on a few pounds. But I have to say Marie's cooking is irresistible."

Leah grinned. "I remember our old argument. You think Italian cooking is best."

"Ah yes. But I've come to change my mind. The French are masters at making the sauces that makes all the difference in the food. The Italian undoubtedly comes in a close second, but the French are truly masters of the sauce."

That evening after dinner the praise that both Albert and Leah heaped on Marie sent her home blushing from ear to ear. Albert had wheeled in the coffee tray for a second helping of coffee. After he served both of them he settled himself. "Well, my dear, everything is ready. But, and I hope you won't fight me on this, I have set everything up for two weeks hence. I felt that you need some rest and relaxation away from the hospital setting to sort of…" he hesitated, "well, to shall we say, find your equilibrium."

Leah looked like she was about to do battle but then her features softened and she too settled back. "Ah, Albert, you sly old fox. I know what you're thinking. Unfortunately I am fully committed and prepared."

Albert flustered a bit. "I uhhh, I assure you my dear I just want you to have a break from the dreadfully monotonous hospital routine."

"And so it will be, Albert. I appreciated your thoughtfulness and consideration. Two weeks it will be. Meanwhile I will breathe in this marvelous Alpine air and rejuvenate myself."

Albert simply smiled in a self-satisfied sort of way.

Leah took advantage in the lull and was pleased in spite of her eagerness to get on with the surgery and get her life in order. She sat out on the porch and basked in the winter sunshine while Albert and Marie kept her supplied with magazines, hot cocoa and snacks. Like anybody who was truly honest she enjoyed the pampering but of course did not admit it. By the end of the two-week hiatus there was a bloom in her cheeks that had wiped out the pallor of the English hospital stay. But now she was ready.

In the morning Albert introduced her to the chief surgeon, the surgical team and the attendants. She gave him a weak little grin as she followed the surgeons downstairs.

As per doctor's orders Albert couldn't speak to her for the first three or four days.

When he was allowed to visit he was dismayed at her condition. She looked so frail and weak. It's not that he didn't expect this but Leah had always been so vibrant and full of life it was odd to see her as weak as a kitten. Her smile was weak too. "Don't look so down, Albert. I'm OK. You know I'm a tough broad."

"I know," Albert said, with little enthusiasm. "Are you through the critical stage yet?"

"I understand in about a week I should feeling more human."

Albert took her hand and gave it a tender pat. "Good," he said, "now rest. I know nothing about your condition but I know that rest is always in order."

She grinned. "Good old Albert. What would I do without you?"

He had been right. By the end of the following week she was looking and sounding better. Albert brightened at this development.

She improved steadily and one afternoon they were sitting on the deck enjoying the glorious spring sunshine. In the distance and through the still winter bare trees the Matterhorn rose up like a gigantic rock, its famous travel calendar 14 thousand foot peak in the clear right up to the summit.

When Albert detected a shadow of some concern beneath the surface of her beautiful eyes, he at first hid his concern. He sipped his cocoa and said, "Anything bothering you, dear?"

Leah seemed distant. But when she answered she turned to him and was direct. "I've been dreaming."

"Dreams are normal I understand."

"Well, I guess then that they are more like nightmares."

"Not unusual either considering all that you've been through recently. May I ask what these nightmares are about? Do they have a common theme?"

"Well, yes. There is always a man lurking nearby. Whether I am bathing or dressing or anything. He is always behind me."

Albert's brows furrowed. "Is he threatening?"

"That's the strange part. Actually, no. It's just that he's there and seems to be reminding me of something."

"Or someone?" Albert added.

"You mean..."

"Yes. David."

"You mean you think he's haunting me?"

"David wouldn't haunt you. He loved you. He might try to be telling you something. That's the only thing I could see."

"Hmmm, maybe you're right, Albert."

She chewed on that a while before saying. "You might be right, Doctor Freud." A little grin came with the remark.

"One doesn't need to be the famous Austrian to know that we are all grieving David's loss and he is maybe trying to stay alive in your memory. Besides the doctors have warned you that with all this complicated surgery there are bound to be flashbacks to your past. He will probably be with you until you decide to let him go."

He let that sink in before he broached another subject. "As you know we have the best security agents here to patrol the grounds. You've stirred the pot some, there is no way of telling who might show up and wish to do you harm."

She sighed. "You're thorough as always, Albert."

Albert's gaze grew more distant. "What we have not discussed is the role you are determined to play in the interest of justice with that Russian fiend. You, of course, can do nothing for the next year or so."

Leah grinned. "That's alright. He'll still be around. Fiends like him have more than nine lives. And the year will allow me time to figure out how I'm going to get him."

Albert seemed to shrug off the remark.

Leah's voice was determined. "And I am going to get him, Albert."

Chapter Fifteen

Leah sat up in the First Class compartment of the British Airways 777 and stretched her arms. She had just awoken from a restful nap and had accepted a martini offered by the passing steward. They were cruising at thirty five thousand feet. She sipped a martini and watched the passing cumulus.

"We'll be arriving in Cancun on time," said a deep male voice beside her.

"Albert, what would I do without you?"

"Oh I'm sure you'd get along fine."

"Then why didn't you let me go on this gig alone?"

Albert sighed. "I thought you promised that we had settled this and that you wouldn't continue to chastise me about it?"

She grinned. "Did I promise that?"

Taking on a somber tone, Albert said, "You most certainly did. You know my feelings. You are really still too soon out of surgery to be traipsing around the world on the trail of Victor Luchensko. What I meant is that you are mentally and emotionally able but I think you are still too weak physically."

"Says you. I tell you I feel fine. Besides, my father doesn't worry about me as much as you do."

"I'm not your father. And that is not a great comparison towards who has your best interests at heart, your father is deceased."

She raised her martini glass. "A toast to a good man."

She sipped some gin and vermouth. "But I do have your promise that after this trip you won't feel so insecure about me and will have no problem letting me operate on my own?"

"Of course."

It was the way he said it that she did not believe him. He was about shutting her up right now. *I'm afraid I have a permanent bodyguard or nanny or guardian angel, whichever I prefer,* she said to herself.

She was about to say something when Albert said, "Now hush up. We are going to have lunch and I understand that the chef is a genius with Mexican cuisine. He's a native German but an expert in Mexican food I'm told."

Leah cocked her head. "A German? Mexican food?"

"It's a cosmopolitan world, my dear. One day we'll all be simply citizens of the world."

Lunch was as good or better than advertised.

Afterwards they sipped a tangy Mexican wine and relaxed. Albert said, "Now to remind you my friends in MI6 are going to make the intercept if we can pinpoint it. Your detective has informed us that Victor is on the island."

"That is if everything goes as planned and the shipment transfers in Cuba and goes on to Southampton in the UK."

"Correct."

"So what do we do if we run into Victor?"

"As we've discussed, I like to avoid that. Otherwise you're going to have to make up some story about recuperating on the island after your surgery from the car accident. But as I said, I think it would be better if we could avoid him."

"How about disguises?"

Albert sipped some wine and then chewed his lower lip. "The only problem with that is that if he sees through it and he is a very astute man."

Leah interrupted. "Especially when it comes to women."

"Especially," Albert added, "but if he sees through the disguise there is no way that the recuperation story will fly. No, I'd say we don't do that. This way if we are discovered you have a reasonable story. You are recuperating and I am your elderly uncle from England."

"Hah. Elderly," she mimicked.

Albert tried hard but could not suppress a grin.

A half hour before landing Albert seemed to grow tense and very serious.

Leah said, "What's the matter?"

"Oh, I was just thinking. If we could catch the sod this time it would be great. If we don't that means that a shipment of Stinger missiles will get through to the terrorists. And I was reading in this morning's *Times* that the insurgents, as they call them, have brought down two more Coalition helicopters... and with guess what?"

Leah said, "Stinger missiles."

"Righto."

"I see what you mean. I guess Victor's evil goes beyond our personal feud with him. He shouldn't be on this earth but for reasons beyond our poor Alicia and his other female victims."

That evening Leah was sitting at the dressing table in her suite at the Presidente Hotel. The suite was large and airy and done in a Mexican motif. They were on the third floor and the suite had a balcony overlooking the sea. Inca, Aztec and especially Mayan art prevalent in this part of the Yucatan adorned the adobe-like walls and there was some extraordinary sculpture and pottery festooning the rooms in strategic places. The bed was a huge four-poster complete with mosquito netting and exotic bed coverings. Of course, the netting was for effect only.

They had selected the Presidente because it was not one of the hotels that Victor used when he was in Cozumel, at least not according to the information Leah had compiled on her last visit almost a year ago.

Albert had the suite next door to hers and she was dressing for dinner. Leah was wearing a black off the shoulder evening dress that accentuated her stunning figure. From the open balcony she could see that the sun was in its nadir and she had just done the fiftieth brush stroke when she saw a figure in the mirror. He was half hidden by the balcony drapes. She froze. Where had he come from? It couldn't be Albert. Albert didn't play jokes and besides she would have heard him come in had he entered without knocking. Again, that was not Albert.

The figure took a step closer and Leah gripped her hairbrush harder, preparing to do battle. God, the silhouette looked familiar. He took a step closer. Leah whirled around. Only the drapes, moving slightly from the evening breeze greeted her. She advanced cautiously and poked the drapes before checking them out thoroughly. There was nobody in her suite. She gazed vacantly at the empty spot in front of the drapes transfixed by what she had just seen and yet dubious about what she had just seen.

A few minutes later Albert's polite knock broke her self-induced trance. When he saw her, his cheery demeanor turned dark. "What's the matter?" he asked as his eyes panned the room.

"I thought I saw someone in my room." Albert quickly pushed her behind him and again scanned the room, his eyes peering into every nook and cranny. Leah said, "He's gone."

"Let me check." Albert withdrew a small pistol, a Glock, from his inner jacket pocket and checked out the room holding the weapon in the approved and now international police stance. Again he scoured the place poking the weapon into every corner. "Whoever it was, he's gone."

Leah said, "It might not have been anybody, Albert. You know about the things I've been seeing back in Switzerland."

"Yes. It is no doubt more of the same. It's going to be a while before you allow David's spirit to cross over."

"Or if he allows it," she added.

"Yes that too."

Albert selected a table at dinner where Leah's back was to the wall and she could see everyone else in the dining room. The dining room was actually a semi outdoor patio, with the moon-drenched ocean all around. Luckily palm trees abounded and almost every diner was hidden from the next. Leah looked wishful as she sipped her cocktail. Albert said, "A penny?"

"Oh nothing. Beauty always makes one want to live forever. On this gig there's a good chance that might not happen."

Albert grew pensive. "I can't say that I've always seen eye to eye with you and David about this Luchensko thing. In a sense one demeans themselves to get revenge."

"How so?" she said with genuine curiosity.

"Because it lowers one to his level. And that's not a level any decent human being wants to be lowered to."

"But you forget, he's not just our personal scourge, he's now a scourge to all decent mankind with his terrorist activities."

"That's true. But again, that's not really the business of people like us."

Leah sipped. Then she looked over the rim of her glass at the older man. "I disagree Albert it's the business of everybody. That's how evil gets along in this world. Everyone figures it's someone else's business."

Albert lapsed quiet. Dinner came and they occupied themselves with the dining experience offered by the best hotel on Cozumel. Halfway through dessert, Leah stiffened. Albert asked, "What?"

"It's him."

"Him?"

"Victor. Don't turn around. I don't think he's spotted us."

Albert said, "He has never seen me. Put the menu up in front of your face. I will scoot over a bit to cover you."

Leah said, "He's pretty occupied. There is a man and two women with him. He's paying a lot of attention to the woman nearest him."

Albert said, "I am going to stand. You stand at the same time. I will cover you and you can walk back past those palms and we should be out of his line of vision."

They moved carefully as if they had orchestrated the maneuver before and a few minutes later they were out of the dining room and heading for the elevator.

Back in Leah's room, she said, "I know for sure he's not staying here. So we have to assume he's here for the cuisine."

"That may be, but let me put in a call to my man and see if things are going on schedule." He made the call and talked in a kind of hushed tone. When he got off the phone he said, "Nothings changed. The shipment of Stingers is due to go out of here the day after tomorrow. With any luck we can nab Mr. Luchensko with the goods."

"But surely he doesn't physically go along with the delivery."

"Oh no. But if we can put him on or near the boat considering all the other evidence we've put together this past year, it might, just might be enough. But we do need something incriminating. As you know he has been very clever about a paper trail. For all intents and purposes so far it looks like Hector and Manuella are in business for themselves."

Leah's skepticism was plain. "Where could an air hostess from Cuba and a poor Mexican fisherman get the capital to be in the arms business and especially in a business as sophisticated and costly as Stinger missiles?"

"Righto. But as I've said, he's been clever. Most of the stuff we have is open to interpretation and probably won't stand up in a court of law."

"You mean the photos?"

"Yes. We have pictures with Victor and Hector. And Victor and Manuella, which I wonder about."

"Wonder about?"

"Yes. I've had all year to study the photos and I'll tell you those two look a bit too tight, if you ask me. Besides, this Hector fellow seems to be out of her league."

"How so?"

"Oh. Just a touch here or there. Some body language here or there that leans to something else between them besides business."

"Hmm. I never realized what an astute detective you are, Albert."

"Well, I'm going to toddle off to bed. Call me if you need me. And one more thing."

She cocked her head.

"Wear sunglasses and a large sun hat tomorrow. It's pretty hard to spot someone in that rig and it isn't a disguise, but perfectly apropos for the island."

"Will do, Albert. Now don't worry. Off to bed with you. I'll see you in the morning."

Albert headed for the door. Leah said, "By the way, what are we passing ourselves off as? Father and daughter? Sugar daddy and bimbo? What?"

Albert grinned. "You decide, my dear. You decide."

And he was off.

Chapter Sixteen

Albert and Leah were sitting on the patio eating breakfast. Leah was wearing big sunglasses and a straw hat; both were dressed casually. Albert was having an English breakfast of schirred eggs and kipfers with biscuits and Leah was sipping coffee and a croissant. Some fruit sat nearby glistening in the sunlight. The great expanse of the sea was darker than usual because it was rough with snow-white whitecaps frothing on the waves.

Albert said, "I received some intelligence this morning from the private detectives and one communication from my friend in MI6."

Leah sipped coffee. Putting the cup down she said, "Anything more than what we already know?"

"Yes, actually. Most important is that the Stinger shipment is due to leave the island the day after tomorrow. Based on the running time to Cuba I'd say that they will leave about dawn for an arrival in early morning darkness."

"Darkness is necessary?"

"Yes, it seems the Stingers are going aboard a submarine. We haven't been able to figure out whether it is North Korean or Iranian."

"So it's time for us to act. It seems to me that the plan we have in mind should work." She lowered her glasses to the bridge of her nose. "Don't you agree?"

"Yes, my dear, but it is predicated on some information I am waiting for."

"And that is?"

"That is something more on our dear Mr. Luchensko, like more about his background."

"Yes?"

He was interrupted by the signal of Albert's phone, "Hail Brittania." Albert spoke in hushed tones. When he hung up he appeared pleased. "It seems that our Mr. Luchensko was a clandestine officer for KGB in the old days. He was attached to the Soviet Navy. He had a lot to do with providing Soviet patrol boats to the Cubans. He was the technical advisor who taught them how to run them. Deadly craft for their time. Carried Gatling guns and missiles too."

"Interesting."

"Yes, because for our plan to work, at least to its most successful conclusion, Victor must be at the helm of *Manuella* when they are intercepted by either the U.S. Navy or U.S. Coast Guard. If we wind up merely intercepting a load of missiles then at least we score one for the good guys on the War on Terror. But it would be nice to nail that scoundrel, Victor Luchensko."

Leah smiled. "Dear Albert, you're so efficient. What would I do without you?"

Albert tossed off the compliment and said, "OK, so as soon as my man lets me know where Hector and Manuella go this evening we will move into action."

Leah said, "So the detective has seen them go out every Saturday night for a month and expects they will tonight. Even though they have an important mission tomorrow morning?"

"That's what we're counting on. If that doesn't happen then we are going to have to break into Hector and Manuella's house to do our thing."

They went over the plan again. It was quite simple. At some point during the evening, Leah was to drop a pill into Hector's drink. The pill would assure that by morning he would be too ill to operate a boat let alone navigate all the way to Cuba. Hopefully the only one available to take the shipment would be Victor himself.

Leah said, "And we have to trail them."

Albert nodded.

Leah asked, "So you say they usually go to a kind of middle class bar? Not one of the fancy big hotel bars?"

"That's right. I guess Hector doesn't want to appear to be anything but what he is, a poor fisherman. All we can do now is wait until we hear from my man as to where they'll be."

"And you know enough about navigation to trail them to Cuba?"

"The little that I have acquired since my days in the Royal Air Force along with the skipper of the boat I hired, should enable us to stay on their tail and then radio in an intercept when we're ready."

"But we have to be careful to make sure we stay out of Cuban territorial waters. We have to grab them before *Manuella* enters Cuban waters."

"Ahhhh," said Albert. "Therein is the rub. The Cubans, unlike other countries, have decided that their territorial waters extend far beyond what most civilized countries claim."

"Do we know what that is?"

"I don't think it is written into international law because nobody else agrees with it. So what it has evolved into is anything the Cubans deem necessary."

With a wry grin Leah said, "How nice for them."

"Yes. It is going to be tricky. There are more than a thousand miles of Cuban coastline and that's not counting the hundreds of bays and inlets. Or the nearby islands, like the Isle of Pines and the Isle of Youth. I have narrowed it down a bit."

"How so," Leah said.

"By the depths of water. The submarine is going to want to operate underwater as much as possible, I would think. Some of the bays are too shallow."

"Haven't they been using the Isle de Pines? Because there are government facilities on the island."

"That's true. There's one of Castro's most notorious prisons, and some marine coastal installations. But we can't by any means assume they are going there. There may be other considerations. Remember, the Navy has reconnaissance going on from Guantanamo Bay and the Coast Guard is constantly off the island looking for refugees."

Leah thoughtfully poured them both more coffee. "And we're sure we can't lay this whole thing on the U.S. Navy or Coast Guard?"

"Not without absolute proof. And we can't get that. Remember, the U.S. is not interested in any beef with Mr. Castro at this time. If things get hot they may have things rigged so they can dump the Stingers if they are apprehended. And then the U.S. has an international incident on their hands giving Mr. C. more excuses to get help from his liberal U.S. allies."

Leah raised her juice glass. "To success tonight."

Albert raised his and clinked hers. "To success."

That evening after dinner there was a knock on Leah's door. It was Albert. "My contact just called in. They decided on a change of pace tonight. They're at El Mariachi at the El Camino Real Hotel."

"Good. So now I know how to dress. Give me fifteen minutes."

Albert wandered out on the patio while Leah dressed. He lit a cigarette and gazed out at the sun balanced like a huge ball on the horizon. The water was shimmering in various shades as the setting sun glistened off the surface.

When Leah appeared she was dressed chicly. An off the shoulder black sarong type evening dress clung to her hourglass figure. A plain string of black pearls provided all the accessory that she needed.

With a toss of her head, she said, "Ready, sir?"

"Ready my dear." He knew he didn't have to ask her if she had the pills with her. Leah made few mistakes.

They took a cab to the hotel and went straight to the nightclub. It was loud. Typically Mexican, there was a lot of yip yipping and Mexican yiii yiiiing.

By the time their drinks were served the MC had everybody up and doing the Macarena. Leah was first up on the stage and as Albert watched smiling as she was up there in a conga like line, slapping hips and shoulders and everywhere else the MC ordered and if it wasn't for the seriousness of their mission was having a lot of fun.

Leah returned to the table breathless and took a long swig of her Margarita, first licking the salt and raising her glass to Albert. "When in Mexico," she chortled.

Albert too took a hit on his drink, but he was tending to business. He had located Hector and Manuella in a far corner of the room and was already figuring out a strategy to drug his drink.

Leah said, "Poor Hector. He looks a bit out of place here. But his wife seems quite comfortable."

"Yes, that's true and it appears to be what our contacts say about the relationship."

"They look like Matahari and the fisherman to me," Leah said lifting her drink again. "Hector looks like he put on his one and only old shiny gabardine suit. Manuella looks like she just stepped out of *La Femme* magazine. A very unlikely couple. And it doesn't look like Horace is drinking much this evening. He's been nursing one drink all the time we've been here."

"All reports indicate he isn't a heavy drinker. A few beers with his fishing buddies but that's it."

Manuella joined in the line dancing and Macarena but Hector never left the table. Albert was beginning to worry. It was getting late and if the place emptied out it would be even more difficult to get at his drink.

At eleven people began to filter out. Albert said, "I think it's now or never. But what do we do?"

Leah grinned and said, "Get ready." When the Macarena again started up Manuella with a whoop joined the group on stage. Hector just watched.

Leah turned to Albert. "Hector is going to leave his table soon." She got up and headed toward the maitre de station. Albert saw her say something to the tuxedoed maitre de and then watched as a waiter approached Horace and spoke to him. Hector got up and followed the man. In a moment Leah was there and he saw her walk by and drop something in Horace's drink on the table before she rejoined Albert.

Both watched as Hector came back looking a bit puzzled. "What did you do?" Albert asked.

"Just told him there was someone looking for him at the front door."

"Ahhh," Albert murmured. "I hope you got the right drink."

Leah grinned. "I doubt if Manuella drinks Corona," she said referring to the strong local Mexican beer.

"Ahh. I'm sure you're right. I've seen her sipping martinis all evening."

"She's a fun loving gal all right. I don't think she's missed one Macarena."

Leah and Albert left and took up station at a coffee shop across the street. During the height of the winter tourist season the place was open until the early hours of the morning.

About 12:30 Hector and Manuella came out and headed for the docks.

Albert said, "Let's follow discreetly. If I'm right they're heading for the boat. They need an early start in the morning."

They appeared to be right since they did head for the boat. There was a light on in the cabin so the spy team guessed there would be another crew member aboard and available for the trip in the morning.

"Where's our boat?" Leah asked.

"It's owned by a Texan, Buck Buchanan out of Galveston. I had him tie up a couple of boats down the dock. Her name is *Texas Rose*. She's a thirty-eight-foot Sports Fisherman, a splendid little craft if I must say. I've taken the liberty of putting our overnight bags aboard."

"Does he know anything about our mission?"

"He's no rube. He's guessed something. I've paid him half of his fee already and the other half is due when we get back."

"Can we trust him?"

"As much as we can trust anybody I suppose. I had a quick check done on him. I picked him because he seems to be in a bit of a sticky wicket finance wise. People like that are desperate. I figured he was our best bet."

"So we go aboard now and wait for Manuella to leave at first light?"

"Hopefully, Hector won't feel well enough to go to Cuba. I'm sure they need to make that submarine connection and I'm hoping that Victor volunteers for the job. I know he has a lot of experience with small boats and he is no doubt familiar with Cuban waters considering his assignment with the Soviet fleet. And I'm hoping that the shipment is important enough for him to take the helm himself. I can imagine what a dozen Stinger missiles and God knows whatever else he has on board is worth on the black market these days. I'm sure the terrorists are paying top price for this kind of weaponry. I am also hoping that he will be unable to entrust this mission to anyone else considering the sensitivity and also the Cubans won't want to get caught helping the terrorists."

They went aboard. Leah met a sleepy Buck Buchanan on the *Texas Rose* and then she and Albert tried for a few hours sleep.

Chapter Seventeen

It was still dark at 4:45 a.m. Albert was up on the flying bridge nursing a cup of coffee and peering through night vision goggles towards the *Manuella*, several berths away when Leah joined him. She said, "Any movement yet?"

"Yes. A cab pulled up a few minutes ago and if I'm not mistaken, Mr. Luchensko has gone aboard. He was carrying an overnight bag so I'm assuming we are in luck."

"Where's Mr. Buchanan?"

"He's asleep, but I'll wake him when we're ready to go. We're going to have to let him get a good lead on us and follow him with our radar and other navigational equipment. We don't want to appear to be tailing him. We kind of have to figure his course and then set the same course. We have to remain below the horizon in order not to be spotted and that's going to take some tricky sailing."

Leah's grin told him she had no doubt he was up to the task. She poured herself a cup of coffee and watched the sun brighten the marina. Soon she could make out the forest of masts and the spider's web of rigging. Across the street and towards the still dark jungle she could hear the cry of macaws and parrots and other jungle birds. Cozumel was waking up.

When they heard *Manuella's* engine rev up and settle down to a steady burble, Albert woke up Buck. He was a tall, rangy Texan with a slightly balding pate. His hair had been blonde when he had a full head but now was closely cropped. He had bright blue eyes and the crinkly weathered face of the sport fisherman.

He looked tired when he joined them on the lower bridge, but still greeted them with a cheery "Howdy, partners." His eyes made an appraising sweep over Leah who looked lovely in tank top and Bermuda shorts.

Buck poured himself some coffee from the nearby thermos and grinning said, "Now, Mr. Albert, you folks don't look like no drug runners to this old cowboy."

Leah smiled. "I can assure you, Mr. Buch..."

"Buck please. People call me Mr. Buchanan and I think I owe them a bill or something."

"OK, Buck. No, we're not drug runners. Nothing like that. In fact, we're on the side of the good guys."

"Lordy me," he said, scratching his balding pate. "Don't tell me I'm working with the Feds."

"No. No fear. But that doesn't mean we're not the good guys. Please try to trust us, Buck."

"Okay, little lady. I'm with you. In fact, your friend Albert here couldn't have come along at a better time."

Buck caught the sly grins Leah and Albert exchanged. "Or maybe 'ol Albert here knew he couldn't have caught 'ol Buck at a better time?"

Albert said, "I think we should get under way, Skipper. I'm going to suggest a course of north northwest until I get our man on our radar and I can give you a more precise course."

"North northwest huh? Can you tell me if we're going to be going through the Yucatan Channel?"

"Very likely," Albert said, his eyes glued to the radarscope.

About an hour later, Albert called out a course and heading and Buck set the wheel. "Looks like it is gonna be the Yucatan Channel."

"Yes. You're right."

The sun was high in the sky when Leah said, "What do you say about some lunch, fellows. I found some shrimp down in the galley freezer. I make a mean shrimp casserole."

Buck said, "Sounds like some fine cookin, Missy. Can I have a Corona with mine?"

Leah smiled. "I didn't say I'd served it. I'll make it and give a yell when it's ready."

"Yes'm," Buck said grinning.

Leah went below and busied herself with lunch. Albert stayed with the radar and the Global Navigational Device. He watched carefully as the *Manuella* carefully skirted every island along the way. When Leah stopped by on her way to the galley Albert said, "He's being very careful not to come into the territorial jurisdiction of these small islands. He's giving them a wide berth."

"You mean the Caymans and the Dutch islands?"

"Yes."

At lunch, Buck said, "So your quail is gonna perch somewhere on the north coast of Cuba."

Albert lapsed serious. "I never said anything about Cuba."

Buck grinned. "And you didn't know I was broke either and that they was gonna take my boat."

The atmosphere in the small salon was tense for a moment and then Buck broke into a big grin that made him look like a big silly boy. "Now don't go frettin, folks. If you checked a little bit more ole Buck don't shake a man's hand and then throw down on him. I'm in. For whatever. I'm in."

Leah felt that she was a decent judge of character, and without consulting Albert she said, "Buck, you guessed right. We're going to try to do our country some good. That boat up ahead has a load of Stinger missiles heading for the Middle East. If it gets through not only do a lot of Americans get killed but one nasty and evil man will make a lot of money while he thumbs his nose at America."

Buck slowly ratcheted his head from Leah to Albert and back and then with a wide smile said, "I'm in, folks. I'm in. I'm too old to go over there and fight them SOB's but if I can help out here I'm with ya."

Leah let out a sigh of relief. Although she had a feeling that this Texan would prove to be a real American she wasn't entirely sure. Like many contemporary people she was skeptical of some.

Toward dark the seas began to darken and the swells picked up. Buck caught a weather forecast out of Key West, Florida that called for squally conditions in the central Caribbean. He told the others.

Albert said, "It's going to be as rough for him as it is for us and I think this is a bigger better boat than *Manuella*."

Buck's ears perked up. "That's *Manuella* up ahead? The one we're following?"

"Yes," said Leah. "Why?"

"I know that dude. Little Mexican guy name of Hector. Used to drink beer with him and his fishing buddies in town."

"That's him."

"Funny," he muttered.

"What?" Leah asked.

"Doesn't seem like the kind of dude to be mixed up in something like gun running."

Albert said, "Maybe it's his wife who is motivating him."

"Oohh yeah. The classy looking chick. Spanish or something."

"That's Manuella," Leah said.

Grinning, Buck's eyes again took an opportunity to appreciate Leah. "Guess I know what you mean."

The three crewmen of *Texas Rose* took turns sleeping and manning the helm. Buck left word that when they rounded the north tip of Cuba they should let him know. He said the waters were tricky there.

It was still dark on the bridge. Only the soft greenish glow of the navigational instruments lit the space. Albert had been at the wheel when he sent Leah down to wake Buck.

The seas were beginning to get rough. Whitecaps appeared and huge waves washed over their bow. Luckily their course took them directly into the waves and every boatman knew that the only way to navigate through high seas was to steer directly into the waves. If the boat began to slip and got broadside there was a good chance that they would broach.

Soon Buck was fighting the waves. When they cleared the eastern tip of Cuba the waves abated a bit, but were coming at them in the wrong direction. Buck had to work hard to keep going in the right direction and not get broadside to the seas.

As a weak dawn flushed over the wild sea, Albert called out, "I think they are taking refuge behind the lee of that island up ahead. Which one does the chart say it is?"

Buck checked. "It's called Isla San Lucas. I think it's a fishing village."

An hour later, exhausted, the *Texas Rose* dropped anchor in the shelter of a headland on the Isla San Lucas. It was less windy but raining steady now. They could make out the squat lines of *Manuella*. Her rigging and towing winch were distinctive.

Albert said, "Let's hope they don't recognize us."

Buck said, "I think Hector will recognize the *Texas Rose*."

"Let's hope that old Hector is still under the weather."

Buck innocently asked, "How do you know he's under the weather? He's a fisherman. A little weather isn't going to bother him."

When he tried to get an answer from either Leah or Albert they avoided his gaze. Then he said, "You folks are trickier than I thought. You know something."

Leah started to say something when Buck said, "No. Never mind. I probably don't really want to know. Lucky for us though, looks like a lot of other boats are riding out the storm in here. We're just one out of a whole bunch of boats."

Leah agreed. It would be real bad luck if they recognized them. But then that doesn't really tell them anything.

Leah broke out some French bread and made them beef stew from the can. She had hot coffee to wash it all down. They ate heartily and waited for the weather to abate.

An hour or so after dark, they spotted *Manuella* heading for the mouth of the harbor. They were right behind her. As they neared Havana, a decision had to be made. *Manuella*, evidently, had no trouble traversing the Cuban coast so close. But they could not take that chance, so they headed further out to sea and tried to keep contact. Unfortunately, the radar on board wasn't sophisticated enough to do that. They needed to be on a direct angle behind her. Eventually as they pushed south of Havana they lost her.

Albert asked Buck to head north and then turn back towards the coast hoping that the angle would be good to pick up *Manuella* on radar. They got a blip just east of Matanazas, Cuba. Leah asked, "Do you think that's her?"

"Not sure. We'll have to close to find out." But as Buck studied the chart he said, "If I was a gun runner, here's where I'd meet my boat."

"Where?" Leah said.

"There's an archipelago out there. The Sabana Archipelago. Lots of small islands. Not many people around. I'd go there."

Albert said, "That's as good an idea as any. Besides, if they go any further east they'll be coming up on Guantanamo Bay. That won't do them any good. Let's try to get a boat out here from Guantanamo."

"Just like that?" Buck asked.

Albert said, "There have been some arrangements made with the U.S. Navy." He returned to the radio and began broadcasting in code. All eyes aboard scanned the horizon until they were squinting with the strain.

An hour later they were anchored off an island in the Archipelago. They were broadcasting in the open, though still in code.

Two boats appeared almost at once. One was a Cuban missile boat and he was bearing straight down on them. The other wore the gray paint of the U.S. Navy. It looked like a destroyer escort. Through his binoculars Albert saw USS *Boston*. Both arrived abeam of them at the same time.

They were not sure about their status in regards to Cuban territorial waters but they were taking a chance to catch *Manuella*. Albert talked to the CO of the *Boston* on the radio but was told there wasn't anything they could do. They were definitely in Cuban waters. It had been a long shot considering Cuba's odd stance on territorial waters. But unless the United States wanted a confrontation with Cuba the Navy had to back down. All they could do was escort the *Texas Rose* safely out of Cuban waters. And that they did.

Leah asked, "What do you think is going to happen?"

"Well, we didn't catch Mr. Luchensko but I doubt the Navy is going to let that sub go unmolested all the way to the Middle East. If they are smart they'll either dump the Stingers or store them on the island for another try later. I think all we did was buy some time for the good guys."

Buck had poured them all a shot of whiskey and as he handed them out he announced, "Shoot, guys. It ain't every day that you can slow down the bad guys. We at least did sumpin out here."

Leah gripped the handrail. "Victor," she muttered under her breath. "One day soon, you will be mine."

Chapter Eighteen

Albert and Leah were morose on the trip back to Cozumel. Leah especially. Albert tried to temper her disappointment by offering, "At least that shipment of missiles won't be going anywhere for a while. They'll have that sub under observation."

She nodded without enthusiasm and went back to her mood. Buck, sensing their disappointment kept to himself.

It was dawn the next morning and the sun was brightening the horizon, and as they pulled into the harbor a sheen of pink light had lit up the water and it began to sparkle. The seagulls sailed above in lazy circles, squawking to one another, prepared to get their breakfast from the incoming fishing boats.

Texas Rose was at the dock by brunch and all tied up. In the forward lounge Albert thanked Buck and paid him off. The Texan offered his services if they needed him again. Albert advised that he wasn't sure but thanked him for the offer.

Albert suggested lunch but Leah begged off. Before they parted, having no particular plans for the day, Albert said, "We'll get him. We just had some bad luck out there. Events got away from us."

At dinnertime Albert called Leah's suite and cajoled her into having some dinner with him. As she sat at the dressing table applying make-up she had the cloying sensation that she was not alone. She watched the mirror as she worked. It was dusk and the room was shadowy. She thought she saw movement, but then dismissed it. For some reason the presence was not disturbing. It was rather benign instead. Before she looked up full she caught the image of a male behind her. Oddly, she was not startled. Not even when she felt the hand on her shoulder. She thought she heard a comforting voice and then it was gone. She let out a deep sigh and finished her make-up.

Albert tried to brighten up dinner by ordering what he knew was her favorite wine, but she only sipped it without much conversation. He respected her serenity. When she spoke she told him about the incident in the room in every detail.

"What do you think?" he asked.

"David. No doubt about it. He knew I was down about our misadventure and he was here to comfort me."

"I agree. Our David is looking after you." They lapsed quiet and turned to their dinner.

Albert was wiping his chin with the linen napkin when he caught Leah gazing at him. "What?" he asked.

"I think it would be easier if I just snuck up on him and did the deed with my Glock 9 millimeter."

Albert thoughtfully sipped some wine. "You could."

She looked up from her glass at him. "But?"

"But how would you like yourself for it?"

Leah's lips tightened. "Have you forgotten what he did to Alicia?"

"No. Not at all. That's why I'm out here trying to do him in."

"Then what difference does it make how he dies. We know we'll save a lot of lives if he departs this planet."

"True. All true of course."

"Then what?"

"I'm just concerned about your moral center. I don't want you harboring this hollow feeling of having done something dark."

"He's dark. He's evil. I won't have any problem with my conscience."

"I respect that. And whatever you decide to do. After all, we did try it my way and we failed."

"Well," she said, her jaw firm, "tonight I'll get him."

Albert hesitated. "You have a plan?"

"Not yet, but I'm working on it."

"Okay, let me know when you have something."

"It will no doubt be a one man job, Albert."

"You always need back-up."

She saw that she was not going to be able to dissuade him so she accepted his input.

Albert was eager after dinner to hear her plan. As they waited for their cocktails he asked, "Well?"

"Nothing elaborate. I'm just going to get into his room somehow, or find a way to be there when he goes to his room and bang. It's over."

"What about his bodyguards?"

"What about them?"

"If they get in my way they go with him."

"Wouldn't it be better to catch him alone?"

She could see the concern and the skepticism in his eyes. She answered, carefully. "Of course. But we both know that's probably not going to happen."

"Well, let me know when you develop a plan."

It was the evening of the next day. About nine o'clock Leah called Albert. "Let's go over to his hotel and see if he's around."

"OK. Do you have some kind of disguise?"

"I've got a wig and I can alter my face with make-up."

"Good. I'll meet you downstairs in what? Twenty minutes?"

An hour later they were at one of the bars at Victor's hotel. Albert made a pretense to call his room and learned that he wasn't in. The desk clerk wouldn't give him the room number, but Leah remembered from her previous excursion to the island that it was one of the two Presidential Suites. She told Albert this and he called again and asked if he could rent the Presidential Suite. Yes, they told him, one is available but when they told him the price, Albert feigned shock and told them he changed his mind.

Leah said, "The Presidential Suites are on the twelfth floor."

A few minutes later, when they got there, she said, "I'm going to fake my way into his room. When I do, you hide out. I'll call you on the cell phone using the vibration feature when I need you. We'll know how many bodyguards and where they will be stationed by then."

Albert nodded and whispered, "Be careful," and then he moved out of sight and Leah took the elevator up.

There was a single maid working from a cleaning cart and cleaning what had to be Victor's room. She approached the women and in good Spanish said, "Senora. I want to surprise my boyfriend, Mr. Luchensko. Could you let me into his room? I want to see his face when he sees me in bed." She fingered a hundred dollar bill as she spoke.

The maid stared at the money, her eyes registering what she was thinking. "No, no, Senorita, I cannot. I will lose my job."

"Nobody needs to know. I won't tell. He is a fun-loving sort; he won't say anything. He'll be so happy to see me."

Leah pulled out another hundred-dollar bill. She knew the wage scale in Mexico was far below the minimum wage of the States, probably around two dollars an hour. The maid's eyes were bright now. She was most likely imagining what she could do with all that money. She said, "Please, Senora. I don't want more money. I am afraid."

Leah pushed the two bills into her hand and said, "Just busy yourself and don't notice me." As the woman was staring at the money Leah slipped into the room. The maid was now beyond enticement, she was hooked and could no more resist the money than she could stop breathing. Money had a powerful effect on poor Third World country types. Leah stayed in the bathroom as the maid finished up cleaning the room.

After the maid left, there was a soft tap on the door. It was Albert.

"Very nicely done. Now what?"

"I'll wait in the closet until the bodyguards leave. I have a silencer on my Glock."

Albert's face was grim. "I'll hide in the maintenance room next door till they come in. I'll see to the bodyguards."

She nodded and the plan was set in motion. In the closet she hid behind Victor's array of Armani suits lined up on the hangers. She even found a footstool she could stand on and not be seen at all behind the clothes.

It was a long wait and difficult to do. Waiting was always more difficult than action. Much more difficult. She preferred the actual action to the nerve-racking wait. At least adrenalin would take care of the action part.

Leah was dozing when she heard footsteps at the door. She checked her watch. It was two a.m. The swinging Victor was being true to his lifestyle and partying to the wee hours of the morning, although both Albert and Leah were certain now that he knew somebody was after him he would be more careful. But she probably could count on him being drunk too. That should put a crimp in his protective senses. At least she hoped so.

The voices were deep. Three men. She heard Victor's voice. The men checked out the room. When the closet door opened she held the Glock in front of her and held her breath too. Light filled the closet and she felt like a spotlight was on her.

She was still holding her breath when the closet door closed. About ten minutes later she heard snoring. With the stealth of a moving shadow she eased open the closet door and inched her way towards the bedroom. Then she heard the snoring again and it wasn't coming from the bedroom. It was coming from a chair near the window. In the dim moonlight flooding in from the balcony she made out a man in a lounge chair. He had made himself comfortable and was sleeping. She couldn't know for sure but she guessed it was the bodyguard and that the other one was no doubt outside the door. She pressed the vibrator button on her cell phone already programmed to call Albert's phone. Then she crept toward the sleeping man. When she was directly behind him she raised the Glock's butt up and using two hands brought it smashing down on the bodyguard's head. Thankfully, there was no outcry, but rather he slumped quietly to the thickly carpeted floor.

Then she proceeded towards the bedroom. Someone was in bed snoring. She wondered if she should double check that it was him. She only gave it a moment's thought and crept forward to check out his face. It was him. She raised the Glock. Aimed. Sweat broke out on her face. A noise at the front door startled her. She turned and headed for it. As she arrived the door opened a crack. She stepped aside, her back to the wall next to the door. The door creaked slightly as it opened further. She smelled Albert's cologne and heaved a sigh of relief. She stepped out. The other bodyguard was on the floor in the hallway, his chair still against the wall.

Albert hissed, "Be quick. The stairway will be best." Both darted for the doorway labeled EXIT and scrambled down the stairs.

They were panting when they slammed the door closed in Leah's suite. Albert said, "Thank goodness, that's over."

He caught Leah's eyes and saw it there. He waited a moment and then said, "You didn't do it?"

"No," she said, "I lost my chance."

"I see," he said, a whole message encapsulated in the two words.

"Well, I see your man was only knocked out."

"That's true," Albert said. "That is true."

Leah poured them two drinks from the sideboard and both gratefully belted it down. Albert said, "There will be another time."

She poured another pair of drinks.

Chapter Nineteen

In the morning Albert rapped on Leah's door. She was already up and dressed in tank top and Bermuda shorts. Albert didn't look his dapper self but was a bit ragged at the edges. Leah said, "Would some breakfast fix you up?"

"I doubt it, but I'd like to have something."

"I'll order up several things from Room Service. We can pick on it."

As they munched whole-wheat toast spread with strawberry jam and sipped strong black coffee Leah said, "Do you think your guy saw you?"

"I doubt it. I came up behind him. How about you?"

"Same. But I still think we'll be too hot here. We have to leave."

"Any ideas?"

Leah slowly buttered some toast. She said, "I learned something about myself last night."

"And?"

"I couldn't do it. Not in cold blood."

"I understand."

"But," she said, rather defensively, "that doesn't mean I don't intend to put him away. And if he had awoken and came after me I would have no trouble defending myself."

"I know," he said. No more needed to be said on the issue.

They ate in silence for a bit, then Albert said, "How about this for an idea. We go to New York and see if he shows up there. In any case, whether he does or not, it would be best he doesn't spot us down here. Hopefully he will think that they just got unlucky the other night and ran into a Navy patrol out of Guantanamo Bay."

Leah was listening intently.

Albert said, "I'll have my local PI follow him and see what flight he boards. When we know where he is we can make plans."

"Sounds good, Albert." They finished breakfast and called the airport. Before Albert left for his own room to pack Leah touched his coat sleeve. "Albert, I know I was all eager to do this myself but I have to tell you, I'm glad you're here with me."

He smiled, patted her hand and left.

They took a cab from Kennedy Airport directly to the Plaza Hotel and booked separate suites. "See you at dinner," Albert said as they parted.

Leah seemed tired and distracted at dinner. Albert, in his most uplifting voice said, "Well, it can't be said that we did no good down there. It seems that the shipment wasn't going to go aboard the sub with the U. S. Navy offshore waiting to track it."

"Good, I needed some good news."

"Of course that's not to say that they can't store them and transship them over at a more opportune time."

"Of course.'

"There's more. Evidently they had no idea we were trailing them since they are still communicating using the code you broke."

"So, has something else turned up?"

"The Stingers didn't get through but they are going to try something else. Mr. Luchensko is getting into the big leagues. My man at MI6 says that dear Victor is going to try something more spectacular than the Stingers."

"What's that?" she asked leaning forward, her interest piqued.

"Well, the Brits aren't entirely sure because even though the messages are in a code we know about they are being super cautious. The British spook types though, have a suspicion."

"Of what?"

"You know the suitcase sized nukes the Russians have been missing for years?"

"Yes?"

"They think they might be selling one to the terrorists."

"What?" She put her wine glass down. "Any more details?"

"None. Like most intelligence gathering work a lot of it is speculation based partly on what they know and partly on what they guess. It's what they call a rather sticky wicket at the moment. They are keeping track of it but know nothing more."

"My God! It's incredible to think what they can due with a nuke. Incredible! Damn. I wish I had done what I set out to do and wiped that scoundrel off the earth."

"Yes, if he were the only one behind the plot. But we have no way of knowing if he has partners and to what extent they are involved."

Leah lapsed thoughtful. "Tell me, Albert. Do your friends in British Intelligence have any suggestions or a mission for us?"

Albert's eyes widened. "Lord no. I'm working with them in a most inappropriate way. They are going out on a limb for me. No. They consider us and we should consider ourselves freelancers."

"So what do you think should be next for us?"

"All I can suggest is play it by ear and see if we can develop a plan to thwart him and put him away for good."

Albert was at her door with news the next morning. "He's in New York. He checked into his usual suite at the Plaza last night."

"Ah," she said. "Have you had breakfast yet?"

"No," I was hoping you would join me."

"Room service or the café?"

"How about the café?" Noticing she was still working on her hair, he added, "Can I meet you downstairs? A half hour?"

"Yes, that would be good."

He was on his second cup of coffee when she arrived. After she ordered, she asked, "Anything new?"

"No."

She sipped her coffee and began cautiously as if she knew his reaction in advance. "What if I begin to haunt his regular night spots. I'm bound to run into him and since he shouldn't suspect me or us he might want to take up with me. He is a braggart. I know that. He might just divulge something."

Albert didn't answer.

She said, "I know what you're thinking. But you have to know that was my plan before my accident. I don't like it either but I think I was making progress."

"Isn't there another way?"

"Can you think of one?"

Again Albert went silent. They finished their breakfast and agreed to meet again at dinner.

Leah was dressed provocatively at dinner and Albert knew that she had made up her mind. He said, "Where are you going to try?"

"Club 54. First."

"Do you have a role for me in this?"

"I'd like for you to cover my back in any way you find appropriate."

He nodded reluctantly, his disapproval obvious.

The club was its usual pounding cacophony complete with the strobe lights and the twisting writhing mass of humanity on the dance floor, each person looking for their own nirvana.

Leah nursed her drink at the bar and tried very hard to look like she wasn't searching for anybody. She had several offers, all of which she politely declined.

She was about to give up when Victor arrived with his entourage, who immediately took up positions either guarding him or serving him. Rather than wait he dispatched one to the bar for a bottle of his favorite elixir.

Leah turned sideways on the bar stool and crossed her legs. About five minutes later a man was tapping on her shoulder and pointing at Victor, whose broad smile reached across the room. He summoned her and she took her drink and moved towards him making sure to use her most sexy stride.

Victor seemed truly pleased to see her and better still when she sat down and let him pour her a drink he didn't seem the least bit suspicious. He said, "It's so good to see you. You look wonderful. Can I ask where have you been this past year? I have looked for you."

She grinned. "So you hadn't heard about my accident?"

"No," he said, with seemingly genuine alarm. "What happened?"

"I was in a bad car accident in England. I've spent the last year having operations and recuperating."

Victor's eyes roamed over her. "My God, your doctors must be miracle workers. I don't see a mark on you."

"It's true they are the best in the world. And I was lucky."

"Are you living in New York now?"

"No. I still spend most of my time in Europe."

"I haven't seen you at Monte Carlo or at Nice," he said, his tone now somewhat cautious.

"Those aren't places I frequent. But I'm glad to see you haven't forgotten me."

"Hardly," he said with a wry grin. "Hardly." With a glance he added, "However I did hear about the unfortunate demise of your friend. I forget his name now."

"David. David McAllister."

"Ah yes. I'm so sorry for your loss."

"Thank you."

She took a fresh tack. "So, what new and exciting has happened to you since I've been out of circulation?"

"Nothing really. A few trips out of town is all."

"Really? Someplace exciting I hope."

He grinned again. "Nothing is as exciting as New York. No, I went to Mexico."

"What do you do there?"

"Some deep sea fishing. Some diving. Relax mostly."

"Ah. I see."

"I'll bet you did?"

Caught off guard, Leah asked, "What? What do you mean?"

He gazed at her, his green eyes twinkling with mischief. "I just mean that I'll bet you wondered about me. Such a beautiful woman, I'm sure you have the attention of every male you are near."

Now she grinned, this time in relief. He had sounded like he knew something. In fact, she still wasn't sure if he didn't know something. She thought this might be a good time to leave. Leave Mr. Luchensko with just enough of her to be teased, aroused and hopefully, vulnerable. She quickly said her goodbyes, although the Russian protested vigorously. Before he could dissuade her she was off. He watched her go, his eyes filled with lust.

Chapter Twenty

Albert's eyes probed hers at breakfast. He wasn't at all pleased with the role that Leah had designated for him. He knew there were going to be situations where he couldn't cover her back and this made him uncomfortable. "Did you learn anything last night?"

Leah took a dainty bite of her wafer thin toast. She grinned. "Only that Victor still loves me."

Albert grimaced. "Look…Leah." She could see he was troubled. "Maybe, down in Mexico you weren't able to do the sod in but that doesn't me I can't."

She bit another piece of toast. "Yes, my deal, Albert. That would probably make it easier all around. But now we have to think about what he is up to. Even if we dispose of him, New York is in doubt going to see its next 9-11."

Albert couldn't argue with that. He said, "So what's next?"

Now it was her turn to study him as he sipped coffee. She said, "I see you are getting used to coffee."

"Ah yes, but it's just a habit. I still prefer tea."

Leah flashed a smile. "We'll make an American of you yet."

He knew she was taking the tension off and that she had something to tell him that he wasn't going to like. Again he said, "So? What is next?"

"I have a date tonight."

"I thought you walked out on him last night."

"I did. But he found me. I had a courier delivered message this morning. His limo is picking me up at eight. Unless my return message was no."

"And?"

"I'll be ready tonight."

"Do you have a plan?"

"Other than trying to gain his confidence? No. But that's enough of a task at the moment."

Albert began staring at his cooling coffee. "I uh don't like to pry my dear, but I must bring up a delicate subject."

She leveled her gaze at him. "How far am I willing to go?"

"Ah. Yes."

"As far as I have to gain his confidence. This thing is a lot bigger than us and our revenge on Victor Luchensko."

"I know. I think I preferred the simpler task."

"I know what you mean."

That evening at eight Albert watched from behind a large pillar near the front door of the hotel lobby as Leah clambered into a long gray stretch limo in front of the hotel. He was out front in a flash and into a cab

He waited outside a popular New York restaurant for two hours while they were inside. Then he followed them back to Victor's hotel.

In Victor's suite, he ordered Room Service and a split of champagne and an array of hors d'eouves. Leah sat on a comfortable single chair and crossed her legs in a whisper of silk. She watched as Victor dispatched his two bodyguards. She recognized one as the one she clonked in Mexico.

When he joined her Room Service had already delivered and had been checked out by the front door bodyguard. As Victor poured champagne he watched the twinkle in Leah's eyes and was curious. He handed her a glass of champagne. He said, "It's Russian. Probably different from what you are used to."

"Not really," she said, accepting the glass. As she sipped, she continued, "See, you are only guessing about me. You know very little."

He smiled and said, "That is the reason for this evening. I want to learn more about you."

"And I you," she said, as she raised the glass in a toast. He gave her his best, most charming smile as he matched her toast and took a sip. He set the glass down. "Now, what is that arrogant little twinkle in your eyes."

"Do you have any clues?"

"Only that I first noticed it when my bodyguard went to take up his station outside the door."

"Very intuitive, Victor. Very intuitive."

"And? You don't like the bodyguard."

"His presence means nothing to me. I just wonder what a man needs so much protection for."

He smirked. "Maybe for a man in a dangerous profession two bodyguards isn't so much protection."

He watched her smile and he didn't like it. "So, you don't think much of a man who needs protection?"

"Bingo," she said.

"Ah, you Americans. Such bravado. What do you know of my position?"

"Nothing. It's one of the things I hope to learn."

Now it was his turn to grin. "I believe you Americans have a saying. Don't hope too much for things. You might get them."

"Ah, I see you are becoming an American."

He laughed. "Hardly. What you see before you my dear is the soul of a Russian. Through and through."

"Ah," she said as she took another hit on the champagne. "So this Russian with all the soul needs bodyguards?"

She could see the irritation in his eyes although he masked it well. "I don't fear for myself personally. I just have a very responsible position."

"I see," she said with utter contempt in the words.

"You think I need them?"

"I certainly don't."

Looking a bit miffed he went to the door and said something to the bodyguard. She heard a hushed protest from the bodyguard and Victor returned. "He's gone."

"You don't have to do that for me. Besides, he's probably nearby."

"No. I dismissed him and his partner for the evening."

She looked over the rim of her glass at him. There was skepticism in her beautiful green eyes. He said, "You don't believe me?"

"Don't worry about it."

"No," he said firmly. "I don't want you to think I am in such fear that I need them."

Leah, even more casually now, said, "Don't worry about it."

He was picking at the finger food and sipping champagne. Things seemed to settle down a bit. Leah said, "So, before you attempt to jump my bones, tell me something about Victor Luchensko."

He looked puzzled. "Jump your…?" Then he smiled. You Americans. I will never learn all your little, uh, what do you call them?"

"Americanisms," she offered with a smile.

"Ah yes. You are American aren't you"

"That's what the passport says darling."

Victor watched as the smile spread over Leah's face, unsure that he had learned anything about this mysterious lady.

"You certainly make an effort not to try to be an American. The Russian distinction seems important to you."

He looked at her. "It is."

"Then why do you spend so much time over here?"

"As I said, New York is the most exciting city in the world."

"You prefer it even after 9-11?"

"Oh yes. That hasn't changed the town too much. Oh yes, you Americans are a bit more paranoid now. But that is to be expected. After all, you have not seen much of the suffering of this world."

"You don't think so?"

"Good grief no. You Americans were so shocked by 9-11 you think it was the end of the world."

"And you of course, you think it was small potatoes?"

"My dear, you are talking to a Russian. We lost thirty million people in the War. And that includes civilians. What did America lose? A couple of hundred thousand soldiers?"

Leah gazed at him. "Many of those dead Russians were at the hands of your own dictator, Josef Stalin."

"True. But he was a visionary. He knew what the Russian people needed. Even if they didn't."

"And that was annihilation?"

He grinned. "That's not what I mean. We were a backward agrarian society back then. We needed modernization, industrialization. All Stalin did was drag the Russians, although kicking and screaming, into the twentieth century."

"So, I've finally found one."

He looked at her, puzzled. She said, "Someone who thought comrade Stalin was a good egg."

He said, "I simply said he was a realist. He knew who his enemies were. And for the most part, despite his paranoia, he was right."

They lapsed quiet until he said, "You are amazing."

"Why? Because I like to talk about the world?"

"Not only that, but that a woman as beautiful as you cares about the world."

"Because the only thing other beautiful women you have known care about is their hair and their nails?"

He grinned broadly. "Frankly. Yes."

She sipped more champagne, and smacked her lips. "Your Russian champagne is very good."

"Many things about Russia are very good."

"Now there's a defensive attitude if I'm not mistaken."

He was doing more smiling than frowning at this point and suppressing a grin he said, "You think Russia is down. And that is true. For the moment. But I can assure you one day she will retake her rightful place in the world."

"And what is that?"

He looked at her blankly. "I mean beyond the Cold War missiles and so forth."

"Okay, I believe you. But what is her rightful place?"

He lapsed pensive. "Compared to most Europeans, you Americans are culturally inferior. But compared to Russians, you are not even in the same league."

"For instance."

"Take art, ballet. Even athletics. For years we Russians were the best in the world at all those things."

"Didn't some of that expertise have something to do with the need for the Russian state to shine in the world? Weren't many of your supposed best amateur artists and athletes, really professionals who spent a lifetime to perfect their art purely for the glory of the Soviet Union?"

He set his glass down and stared at her. "You really are a cosmopolitan person, aren't you. I can see you know more than what would come from some reading."

"I try to keep an open mind."

He took her hand and led her to a love seat, where he plopped down with her. She had the champagne glass in her hand and he took it from her and set it down on an end table. He leaned over and kissed her. She didn't resist. Moments later they were kissing passionately, their tongues swimming back and forth. Leah moaned. He almost panted at the sensations. He leaned over and dimmed the light. The fire in the fireplace cast an erotic glow over the place. Victor was removing his tie when Leah reached for his crotch. He gasped. Moments later he was staring at the back of her head and gasping with delight. Holding her mane of hair he muttered, "No. Don't. Stop."

But it was too late. His body writhed in a great convulsion and he collapsed back in the chair. Minutes later he was snoring and Leah tiptoed to the door.

As she got in the elevator, a man behind an open newspaper put it down and got in with her. "Everything all right?" he asked.

Leah grinned. "Yes, the knock-out pill worked fine. And it fit easily into my ring," she said, flashing the large emerald ring she was wearing on her right hand.

"Good."

"Albert. I haven't been supervised on a date for years now. Yes, everything is fine."

They parted when they emerged from the elevator. Albert murmured, "I'll see you back at the hotel. We should take separate cabs."

"OK, Daddy."

He frowned and headed for the front door. Leah followed. She noticed the two bodyguards on a couch in the lobby. One was dozing. The other seemed to be lost in his newspaper.

Chapter Twenty-One

Leah was sitting across from Victor at a corner table in the Russian Tea Room. She noticed that it was the same table as their previous meetings. He must either be important or have a lot of money. Or both, she thought. She looked ravishing in a black off the shoulder silk Armani dress, which was casual for the Tea Room. Victor was dressed like the playboy he appeared to be. Blue blazer, white scarf and Bruno Malei loafers. He was toying with his wine glass and gazing at her. Little had been said so far, and nothing about the previous evening. Leah said, "You look like you're dying to ask something."

"Ah, so perceptive. As usual."

"I'll go a step further."

"Yes?"

"About last night."

He grinned. "I am so obvious. Lucky I'm not in the spy business."

She smiled back. "Yeah, lucky." She lowered eyes in the most alluring manner and then looked up over her wine glass rim at him. "You want a report card?"

He backed off, looking nervous. "No, of course not. After all, I am a gentleman." But he still looked uncomfortable. "I am afraid I went to sleep early; that is not like me. I do apologize."

"For what? If you're worrying about performance before you zoned out…"

She watched him squirm a bit as he tried to be casual, but there was urgency in his eyes.

Letting the tension build she stirred her martini carefully. When she looked up she said, "I find that men tend to get even more arrogant and conceited if they are fawned over by women."

He took a hit of his drink. "I can't see you fawning over anybody."

She again lowered her lashes, prolonging his curiosity. "It seems we are getting acquainted then." She sipped the martini. "Oh for God's sakes relax. You were wonderful. A stallion."

He grinned. "I wasn't looking for…"

"Well then, even if you weren't you've got it. And if you want to go to dinner tonight I'm available."

He frowned. "I have to fly to England this evening."

She said, "Oh well."

He lapsed deep in thought. "I'll tell you what. I'll have my limo come by about seven. We can have an early dinner and be at the flight by 9:30."

She made him wait for the answer. "No."

"No? That's all?"

"I said, we are just getting acquainted but you don't know all that much about me. I'm not some bimbo you can trot around the world whenever you feel the need."

He almost sputtered in protest. "I can assure you that I…"

"Yeah sure. You think of me as something special."

"But I do."

"Again, I don't follow you around the world serving as your plaything."

"No. I thought we could take in some of the wonderful London night life."

"I have a townhouse in London. I've seen them all."

"Well, I'm sure there are other things. I am sure I can show you a good time."

Leah laughed. "Now there's a wrong assumption in the acquaintance process. You assume I, like most of your girlfriends, are only looking for a good time."

That seemed to really perplex him. He looked at her, jaw agape, thinking hard of some comeback. He said, "Let me try to find out what you want."

"How long are you going to be in London?" she asked.

"I'll be at the Plaza. Probably five or six days."

"Will you be leaving London?"

"Yes, I have to go up north for a day or so. I...."

Leah finished her martini and stood up. He stood too, looking expectant. She said, "Tell you what. I can't see you today anyway. But I will meet you at the Plaza later on this week."

As she walked off he seemed to gaze at her in wonder. Then he called out, "I'll see you in London."

Albert was intrigued by the news. "Up north huh," he said. "Probably his Manchester connections. Do you think I should put my friends on it?"

"What do you think?"

Albert's brows knitted together. "Do you know what I think? When the cops aren't 100 percent behind something they will muck it up. And right now they are not entirely sold on this."

"Just like here. Plus there's the inter agency problems. So you think we should follow this up ourselves."

"Yes. Yes indeed," he replied. "We can always call for help over there if we need it."

"He's leaving tonight and I promised to meet him Thursday night. We need to leave tonight too."

"Private charters?"

"Yes, if we don't we might run into him."

"Unless we take another airline," Albert suggested.

"I suppose we could if we can't get a private charter. But let's first try the charter."

Within an hour a private charter company offered them space on a private flight. It was a Corporation that liked to save money by carrying any other passengers wealthy enough to tag along. They booked it and found themselves at Heathrow on Wednesday morning, sleepy and hungry.

They checked in to the Plaza under aliases and had some breakfast sent up. As they munched on English biscuits and tea Albert sighed in delight. Leah grinned. "Nothing like home cooking, huh?'

"Ah yes." He wiped his lips and then put in a call to Victor's room. And with his authentic British accent was able to beg off as a mistaken room service call. He had the room number. It was two floors below them.

Albert studied the street below as Leah changed into comfortable clothes. When she re-appeared he said, "I think we should loiter in the coffee shop across the street. It has a good view of the hotel's front door. We can move when they do."

Leah readily agreed. She then slipped on her large hat and sunglasses and changed into a plain black dress, which was dowdy and would therefore make a good enough disguise.

As they sipped coffee a black BMW limo pulled up in front of the hotel. Albert quickly headed for it. He approached the driver, who was dressed in a black livery uniform, he asked, "Excuse me, old chap. Is this limo for Mr. Vichinski?"

The driver said, "Mr. Vichinski? Sounds familiar," he added as he fished a sheet of paper from his inside jacket pocket. He perused it and said, "It's for a Mr. Victor Luchensko, party of four."

"Oh, sorry," Albert said, as he moved around to the rear of the car. The driver was already back inside the vehicle when Albert dropped to one knee at the rear of the car to tie his shoe and secured a GPS device under the rear bumper.

Back at the coffee shop he said, "Mission accomplished. Now the thing for us to do is get a car."

Leah said, "If we both go we might lose him."

"That's true, but the device should put us right back onto them. Besides, you can't do much sitting here."

Leah grinned. "I bow, sir, to superior sleuthing."

Albert was already on his way to the National Car Rental booth in the hotel lobby. Sure enough, before he returned Victor and his two bodyguards got in the BMW.

Albert pulled up in front of the coffee shop ten minutes later. Leah quickly got in. "They headed north," she said.

Albert glanced at the GPS monitor in his hand and said, "Looks like they're on the E10."

"That goes to Manchester, doesn't it?"

"Right O," he said, as he maneuvered through the London traffic and barely missing a double decker bus loaded with tourists. After about fifteen minutes of hair-raising driving he was out of the London traffic and heading for the E10.

Leah whistled softly under her breath. "Albert, you're full of surprises. I never knew you were such a wheel man."

"Wheel man?"

She chuckled. "You know...driver."

They made up the lost time on the E-10 and soon were several car lengths behind the limo. If they were bound for Manchester both knew that they had about a two-hour drive to deal with. Leah had thought ahead and had brought along a coffee for herself and a tea for Albert. He sipped his gratefully. "Ah, that hits the spot."

Leah said, "Tell me, Albert, if a suitcase sized Soviet nuke is what they plan to sell what are the logistics about bringing it into the United States?"

"Well, I've been thinking about that. And what I would do if I were them."

She sipped some coffee. "And?"

"Well, first of all I would forgo any form of public transportation. I wouldn't try a cargo ship either. Although you Yanks are terribly behind the curve on the inspection of all ship cargo, there's still a chance that a device already charged could be detected."

"You mean the fissionable material?"

"Exactly. No. What I would do would be to use the very open and very porous US / Canadian border. I understand there are places where one could walk into the States through the woods. I'm told one could do it in Vermont, Maine, in Michigan, in Minnesota and several other places. My person al choice would be Vermont. It's closest to Montreal."

"Because?"

"It's a very sparsely populated state. There are parts of northern Vermont that have never been explored believe it or not. And better still it is very close to New York City, at least relative to those other states."

Leah said, "Albert, I'm impressed. You're way ahead of me on this."

"Depending on what we learn from our trailing of dear Victor, offhand I could see that we should concentrate on flights by non-American carriers into Montreal. Whatever we find out today I'm going to make that my next task. Collect the airline flight schedules at the airline office in the hotel lobby and study them."

Leah was listening intently.

"And," Albert continued, "we do have one lucky break. There won't be as many flights going from say, Manchester or London to Montreal, as there would be to New York."

"That's true, but as I think about it, how possible is it to get something like that, that's going to set off any detection device onto a commercial airliner?"

"Right O," so we're going to have to check into private charters, much like the flight we came in on. They land at separate areas of the airport, but I can see that a little bribe here or there would easily facilitate getting it into Canada."

Albert said, "We can't forget Mexico. Remember, dear Victor has connections down there, although we crimped his tail on his last Mexican adventure."

Chapter Twenty-Two

When Victor and company cruised by the city of Manchester and kept going north Leah and Albert were puzzled. "So much for the Manchester connection," Leah said.

"Not necessarily. They may be going to a suburb or farm." Ten minutes later Albert was proven right as they turned off the main highway onto a secondary road and then onto a country road. The countryside was relatively flat. The last connection was a dirt road leading to a farmhouse that they could see through the meadows and tree lands. They followed slowly until the GPS indicated they had stopped. Albert pulled the car off the road and into the woods.

Leah glanced at her flat shoes and ran a hand over her nylon-clad calf. "Too bad I didn't have time to pack a B bag with some useful things like boots"

Albert said, "Everything is in the trunk."

Leah smiled. "Albert, you are priceless."

He had two B bags in the trunk. Both quickly changed into hiking books and donned their ski masks. Dusk was falling when they were ready to go. Following Albert's lead, Leah also shoved a couple of power candy bars and a flask of water into her backpack. She said to Albert, "Do you have the night vision goggles?"

"Indeed, one pair is in your pack."

They set out for the farmhouse at full dark. In only a few minutes they had to jump into the woods as a vehicle approached going up the dirt road from the farmhouse. It was the limo. And although they couldn't see into the shaded rear windows they had to assume the passengers had been dropped off.

When they arrived at the farmhouse, there was just enough light left to discern that it was a very common type of dwelling, with a barn and a couple of other outbuildings. Farmers in this area grew oats and alfalfa, which was stored in the barn.

Leah and Albert stole up to the edge of the woods. The house was about fifty yards away surrounded by a green lawn. Albert murmured, "A bit odd for a farmhouse, wouldn't you say?"

Leah said, "Yes I would say, it looks like the clearing is to give them sufficient coverage of anyone approaching."

"And a field of fire," Albert added.

There were lights on in the lower floors of the farmhouse. Upstairs, all was dark. In the prone position and using the falling shadows as cover Leah and Albert studied the area through their night glasses. It didn't take them long to ascertain there was a guard pacing off his post around the house. The night glasses revealed him to be a swarthy, bearded man. Leah quipped, "All he needs is a dirty night shirt."

Albert grinned, but cut it short when they hear car tires crunching on the gravel of the dirt road. It was a Mercedes and it pulled up in front of the farmhouse. Leah and Albert studied the four passengers as they alighted. One was a very slender form. Leah said, "Hey. Isn't that Manuella from Mexico?"

Albert whispered, "It certainly is and she is wearing her stewardess uniform."

"Damned if she isn't. Are any of the others Hector?"

"I don't see him. The others all appear to be Middle Eastern types."

Leah looked worried. "We aren't going to be able to get a peek through those windows unless we put the guard to sleep."

"But then they'll know they've been spotted."

She said, "Not if we use a mild knockout drop. I'll bet that rather than report he was asleep for ten minutes, he'll say nothing."

"It's a gamble."

"Want to take it?"

"Indeed," replied Albert. "By all means."

When the two were able to determine when the guard would again appear on this side of the building they dashed up to the side of the house and waited. When he didn't show they peeked around the corner. He was sitting against a tree having a smoke. Albert said, "Maybe it would be better if we just slipped into the basement door without taking a chance on how conscientious this guard is."

"Right."

Minutes later they had tiptoed down a flight of cellar stairs and jimmied the lock. It was pitch black inside. Albert whispered, "The night glasses have another feature. Flip the switch and they are simply night vision glasses."

Leah did as he instructed and they proceeded to check out the cellar. There were a lot of farm implements, wheeled wheat cutters, a small tractor and several unidentifiable tools. Upstairs the drone of several voices could be heard, but they could make nothing out. Some of it was in Arabic. They continued around the cellar until they found what they were looking for in the corner. There was a crate and beside it a couple of cylinders with Russian lettering. Leah had spent part of the last year of her life studying Russian. She grimaced. Albert asked, "What does it say?"

"Danger," she whispered.

"Ah," he said. "Do you think we could lug this stuff out of here?"

"I think the crate maybe, but not the most important part. Those cylinders. I mean, without knowing what we are doing we could kill ourselves handling those. Yeah, we might be able to do it. But not without being caught. I think we should forget that idea."

They stopped whispering for a minute and listened for any sounds in the pitch-blackness of the cellar. Finally Albert said, "Let's go upstairs and see if we can hear anything useful."

"Right."

Albert said, "You go. You know Russian. I'll keep watch."

She nodded and started climbing the stairs, wincing at every squeak, which was exaggerated a thousand fold in her mind. At the top she squatted down and felt a cold draft on her face. The voices were in the next room but she listened intently trying to pick up anything.

A few minutes later, she had rejoined Albert who was keeping watch at the door. Leah said, "Is the guard walking his post?"

"Yes, he is now. He left about one minute ago."

"That gives us about two minutes to make the woods. Shall we go?"

"Have you learned anything?"

"Maybe. But remember, if they catch us, all is lost. It's better we get away when we can than take further chances."

"Exactly right. Let us go." They were up the stairs and dashing for the cover of the woods. When they plopped down in their old positions they had another minute or so before the guard came by.

"What did you find out?"

"I'll tell you back at the car."

Albert didn't immediately agree. "My dear," he said, "in what we are engaged in it is better we both know the same thing; in case one of us gets caught the other will still be able to be useful."

A grinning Leah said, "Why Albert. You dear old fraud. You've done this before."

"Perhaps," he said with a wily smile she couldn't see in the dark.

"OK. They were in the other room so I couldn't hear everything. Even if I could my Russian is only so so. But I dear hear the word Montreal mentioned more than once. I think our guesswork may be right. The best way for them to get that hot item into the States is through Canada."

"That's not saying much for our Canadian friends is it?"

"Well, don't forget Manuella is in on this. I figure it's the Russian Cuban connection. I'll bet there's a Cuban plane waiting for them at Manchester Airport and it's bound for Montreal."

"There's only one way to see if you're right. Follow them."

They went back to the car. Leah's throat was dry so she took some water and ate a power candy bar. Albert did the same. She said, "We could go to Montreal Airport now and see if we can find out anything about a Cuban flight. I know Cuba has flight rights with Canada. They are probably going to cross the US Canada border on foot or on some four wheeled type vehicle. What do you think? Should we try? We might be wrong and lose them."

Albert said, "You're right. We don't have the GPS device to follow anymore. If we lose them here we've lost them."

"But the other side of the argument is we need time to make our own arrangements to get to Montreal. We may be too late if we have to follow them."

Albert took another drink of water. The car was silent, although both of their minds churned busily. Finally Albert said, "I say we go now. We know they are headed for New York. We know that the first stop is Montreal. I say we go now."

Leah shook her head. "I bow to experience my dear Albert."

A pink dawn was flushing out the rural English countryside as they followed the signs for Manchester Airport. They parked the car, shouldered their bags and went in to the international terminal. As Albert ordered them both a hearty breakfast, Leah checked out the counter.

Albert was already eating when she returned. He said, "Sit down, your breakfast will get cold."

She sat and began buttering her toast. "Guess what. There is a charter full of tourists going to Calgary for the rodeo."

"Where's that?"

"Alberta, western Canada. First stop is Montreal."

"Ah. Can we book passage? They don't know me and I think you can disguise yourself well enough."

"Let's see." As she ate she noticed that Albert was having an English breakfast while hers was American. "Albert, you're so thoughtful."

He grinned. After breakfast they went to the Cuban Airlines terminal only to learn that one could not buy passage on a charter. One needed membership in the Manchester Equine Club. Also one needed to book a month ago.

"Damn," Leah grumbled.

Albert said, "We need to try for a private charter." They took an airport cab over to the private charter terminal several miles away. It cost them an extra five hundred dollars to get a reluctant charter company to find a pilot at this time of the morning who wanted to fly to Canada.

They were in the air and gazing down at the Atlantic two hours later and their schedule was about two hours ahead of the Cuban jet.

Before he dozed off Albert said, "Do you think we made the right choice?"

Leah patted his hand. "They said they were going to Montreal. Relax. We made the right choice. Manuella is their passport into Canada. I'm sure they have agents bribed on both sides of the Atlantic to allow them to ship their device."

Albert said, "I hope so."

Leah again patted his arm in a maternal way. "Go to sleep dear Albert. You've done a hell of a job tonight. We'll be up and at it again soon enough." She looked to see his reaction and he was already snoring softly. She curled her head against a pillow, cuddled under the blanket and went off to sleep.

Chapter Twenty-Three

Leah was wolfing down a sandwich as she waited for Albert to return from renting a car. When he arrived she handed him a ham and cheese sandwich and a paper cup of coffee, which he accepted gratefully. Neither of them had eaten since Manchester.

Leah said, "The monitor says the flight is on time and will be here in less than an hour."

Albert wiped his lips with the paper napkin provided and said, "We still have to reconnoiter the airport. I doubt if they are going to try to sneak the device through customs. I'll bet all their dirty arrangements have been made to load it right off the plane"

"I'm sure you are right," Leah said. "I'll wait here in case the flight status changes."

Albert nodded and was off. A half hour later he was back. "Problem," he said.

She cocked her head and waited.

"There are three exits from the field. If we stake out one we might miss them. And we don't even know what kind of vehicle we are looking for."

Leah knew where he was going with this, and finished the thought for him. "And that's also if our guess is right that they won't try to come out with the rest of the passengers through Customs."

"Roger."

Leah said, "As I see it, then, all we can do is get another car. At least that narrows the odds."

"Yes," Albert agreed, "and two of the exits are close by. With any luck and our good field glasses we should be able to spot them. Look, I have a gray Peugeot. Try to rent something distinctly different so we can recognize each other. One will have to follow the other on the road until a good time to pair up."

Leah was back twenty minutes later. "I have a white Renault. We probably should take up our positions out there."

"Roger. Be careful," he said.

Both found their best vantage points and waited. It was tense, as they had to eyeball every single car that emerged from the field exits. Then there was the strain of trying to see who was inside. Albert had to be extra cautious as he was covering two exits and had to use his field glasses.

Leah was starting to worry when she saw a limo bearing diplomatic plates and two small yellow flags on the fenders. She couldn't recall what country they belonged to but she was sure it was Arabic as it had Arabic lettering. She was peering hard when she spotted Victor in the passenger seat. She quickly averted her head as the limo passed. She waited for another car to pulled in behind the limo and took off after them. With one hand she dialed Albert on her cell phone. He said, "I saw you take off after them. That's the deal then. Phony diplomatic car and plates. I'll try to stay a few cars back."

"OK."

Traffic was light this time of night and the sky had begun to weep softly into the dusk. This didn't help visibility and Leah strained to keep them in sight. Before she realized it they were pulled over and she passed them. Quickly she called Albert. "They pulled over."

"Yes," he said, "I passed them too. They're taking off the flags. That's all I could see. Probably changing plates too. I'll pull over where I can and get back behind them without them seeing me."

"I will too."

It took another ten miles but both managed to drop back behind the limo. Leah had noticed a railroad crossing up ahead and as she approached she heard the mournful whistle of a train. *Oh no!* Just as she feared they had crossed in time, but she had to stop and wait. However, it looked like Albert had made it across in time. She tapped her fingers on the steering wheel as the endless line of freight cars rolled slowly by.

When she finally saw the caboose and the end of it she knew she was miles behind. All she could do was step on the gas in hopes of catching up. Signs for the Canadian border with the state of Vermont were now appearing and she feared she had lost them.

When she arrived at the checkpoint she knew she had gone too far, so she did a U turn in the road and headed back looking for any sign of a small country lane or road where they might try to illegally enter the United States. It was now full dark.

After driving over the last three miles back and forth she was beginning to despair when she spotted a car's flashing lights. She pulled up beside it. It was Albert's Peugeot. She got out carefully, pistol in hand, but after a thorough search she found no sign of her companion. But about a hundred yards into the woods she found a small trail heading south. She used her flashlight knowing that her prey and Albert were long gone. Albert had to have left the car to guide her.

Leah set off through the dark wet woods hoping to catch up with Albert. It was slow, miserable work in the dark. Although she had packed her slicker in her backpack her legs were soaked. She stopped and slumped under a tree for a rest and a drink of water. She also took a couple of bites from her Granola bar for energy. She and Albert had discussed the new realities of the situation that morning at the airport. She had told him, "I know I couldn't kill him in cold blood in New York, but things are different now. Millions of innocent lives are at stake and I now have every intention of killing any or all of them."

Albert was somber in his answer. He said, "I feel exactly the same, my dear."

So a pact had been made between them. They were going to stop these people in any way possible, even if it meant killing them in cold blood.

She plodded on for what seemed like hours but her watch told her it was only three hours.

Leah was concentrating so hard on trying to stay on the trail in the dark that she almost bumped into the little cabin. It was more of a shack actually, probably used by hunters on weekend forays. She was about to check it out when a voice warned, "Don't take another step."

She froze, and considered reaching for the Glock in her jacket pocket. The voice spoke again. It was closer. Behind her. And friendly. It was Albert. She whirled around, saw him and hugged him hard. "I thought I'd never catch up with you!" she exclaimed, albeit quietly.

"Well, you have. Now come on in and dry off and get something to eat."

"What? Don't we have to keep on after them?"

She couldn't see it but heard the grin in his voice. "Remember you said to me 'you've done this before?' Well, I have and believe me they won't get far ahead. At this point I'd say they are less than an hour ahead and there's still some bit of wilderness before we come to any civilization. Best to dry out a bit and rest. They're not and that will weaken them."

Inside the cabin, Albert lit a couple of candles and began stoking up some embers in the wood stove. He quickly had a mini meal of hot coffee and baked beans ready. Leah had changed into a dry pair of pants and set her boots and other clothes by the fire to dry. The beans and coffee were as welcome as a gourmet dinner at the Plaza. It seemed to re-energize her. When she got into her dry clothes she was ready for a nap but Albert said, "I'm afraid that's about as much refreshing as we can do. We have to get back on their trail now."

"Do you have any idea where we are?"

"Yes. I picked up some detailed maps at the airport. I'd say we are either already in Vermont or will be soon. Do we have any plan other than catch up with them?"

"I don't. Do you?"

"No," he said, "I guess there will be time enough for that after we catch them."

When they set out again they had picked up the pace. Albert said, "We should spot them soon. They don't know they are being trailed and so they're using their flashlights."

About an hour later they broke into country that was more open with the occasional meadow or field. The woods weren't as thick either. They were crossing a meadow when a shot rang out from the tree line. Albert dropped like dead weight. Leah hit the ground and began a frantic crawl toward him. When she found him he had his finger to his lip. Leah sighed with relief when she saw he wasn't hit. She said, "I thought sure you were hit."

"I dropped like that so that they would think so too. Let's try for that cover," he whispered, pointing at the edge of the tree line about fifty yards away. They did it in a slow infantryman's crawl.

In the cover of the woods they searched with their night glasses. Leah hissed, "There. There they are. At least two of them." She pointed Albert in the right direction.

He said, "Let's try to flank them."

"Crawl behind them?"

"Exactly."

It was a slow, painstaking process but they finally managed to get behind the two terrorists who were still waiting for them from their front. There wasn't much dry wood on the ground due to the recent rain but Leah unfortunately came into contact with some brittle twigs. They snapped under her foot with a loud crack. The terrorists whirled and began firing their AK-47s. The AK is a Russian weapon with a terrific rate of fire. Soon the black woods were lit up with orange and white muzzle flashes. While the terrorists were firing blindly Albert and Leah had the advantage of knowing exactly where they were. Not only from the muzzle flashes, but also from their night vision equipment, so when they began firing their combined shots soon found targets. They heard a couple of yelps and the firing stopped.

They waited at least five minutes and then cautiously, darting from tree to tree, approached the terrorists. They were dead. Albert snatched up one of the AK-47s and a bandolier of ammo and they set out after the rest of the crew, which appeared to be Victor and two or three others.

"These guys must have been rear guards," Leah speculated.

"Yes, I thought that too. But what bothers me is: what alerted them to us at all?"

"Maybe they don't know it's us. Maybe they were just covering their trail. Kill anybody who was in the area. Border Patrol or whoever."

"Yes, maybe you're right," said Albert. "The important thing is we have to realize that they now know we're here. That's why I think we should flank the trail. It'll be light in a couple of hours and the going will be easier. But to use the trail is to invite ambush."

They set out again, this time, super cautious. Dawn was weak and gray, reluctant it seemed, to light up the dark forest. Soon they were approaching a large open field. Albert surmised that if they did the proper thing and skirted it, it would take them several miles out of their way. He further conjectured that the trek would be over soon and if their quarry got to a car and on their way to New York there would be no way he and Leah could find them or stop them. So they headed directly across the field. Luckily the grass was high and a low crouch would keep their silhouettes blurry in the dim morning light.

This time a burst of fire from the wood line took Albert down. But for real. He was hit. When Leah reached him he was gasping; a wound in his upper thigh pumping blood at a ghastly pace. Leah immediately slipped off her backpack, found a pressure bandage and applied it, taping it in place. Between gasps, Albert said, "I don't think it hit the bone. But I still don't think I'll be able to walk."

Leah's diagnosis was, "I agree you can't walk but the hit is only inches from your femoral artery. One could bleed to death in minutes if that's hit. We need to get you help."

Albert gasped hard. "Leah, listen. I'm not being heroic, but millions..."

He was interrupted by another burst of automatic weapons fire. Evidently the terrorists changed tactics and charged. Three men pounded over the meadow towards them. Albert muttered, "The AK."

Leah snatched it and put the three into her sites. A long burst brought down one. The other two began to work their way around to her left. She fired several bursts in the grass where she thought they were. She thought she heard a scream over the chatter of the weapon. But she didn't have much time to think about it. The terrorist, actually one of Victor's bodyguards whom she now recognized, was charging them only a scant few yards away. Leah swung the weapon towards him and pulled the trigger. Nothing happened. He was leveling his weapon now. It looked like an Uzi.

When a shot rang out and large red hole appeared in his forehead and the big man crumpled to the ground in a heap. Albert gasped again and laid back, the smoking pistol still clutched in his hand. A sigh of relief whistled through Leah's teeth. She waited. The woods were quiet. The birds that had scattered when the firing began were settling down now in other trees and chirping and squealing in protest.

Albert's color was bad. He had blanched out sheet white. His voice was weak. "According to my count that leaves only Victor if the yelp we heard was a hit."

Leah said, "Lay quiet. I'm going to find out." Even though Albert started to protest she crawled away. Ten minutes later she was back. "He's dead." But Albert didn't answer. Her own heart pumping, Leah quickly put a finger on the pulse in his neck and waited. Then another sigh of relief. He was still alive. But now. *What to do? God. What to do?*

Chapter Twenty-Four

Leah was in a bind. She knew she couldn't leave Albert, yet, if she didn't, Victor was sure to get to New York City with the nuclear device. She had to evaluate the life of a good friend in comparison to the lives of millions of strangers. Damn. What to do! She chewed her lower lip in frustration.

Albert looked pale. Through clenched teeth he muttered, "You've got to leave me. I'll take my chances. If I keep loosening the tourniquet every hour or so I should be alright."

Leah didn't bother speaking. She simply shook here head. Emphatically.

Albert kept at her. "You've got to get after him. If he makes it to New York they'll turn it into a pile of ashes."

Incredulous, Leah said, "With one little satchel?"

His voice now lower, but still strong, Albert said, "It'll gut the city."

Leah noticed that Albert was beginning to shiver. "You're going into shock," she said. "I have to get you under cover and some food into you."

Before Albert could protest she was off to scour the woods for a crutch. She soon found one with a crook at the end. She brought it back and padded it with a sweater from her pack. Albert was dozing and she had to rouse him. This is what she was worried about, him slipping off into shock. Then she had a good chance of losing him. He had not had a puncture of the femoral artery, but it was close and he had lost a lot of blood.

With some coaxing, she got him up and on his feet. She said, "I'm going to support your good side and let the crutch carry the weight of your wounded leg."

He nodded and they started out. At first the pace was so slow it was hard to measure progress, but eventually they picked it up as they got used to the routine. Leah made sure they stopped every fifteen minutes or so for a rest. So far the countryside had not changed. They were still in deep piney woods with an occasional meadow breaking it up. The land in general was flat. They did notice even the slightest hill, however, as the going was so much harder. Their legs ached and they fought for breath at every incline. At the rise of one little hill Albert was white faced and panting. Leah quickly sat him down and gave him some water. He refused a power candy bar.

It was still early afternoon but Leah had decided to find shelter or make some and give Albert a decent rest. She hacked down some pine boughs for a lean-to and then made Albert a bed out of the boughs. It took her an hour to make the lean-to and heat up some water for the instant cocoa they carried. The cocoa had been Albert's idea. He said it would provide more energy than coffee while still providing the caffeine element. And he was right. Albert was feeling better after a cup of hot cocoa and a half of a Granola bar.

As they sat thinking Albert said, "What would we have to do to attract the attention of authorities?"

Leah said, "I suppose we could fire off some shots, but I hate to use up all of our ammunition in case we meet up with our friend Mr. Luchensko."

"It might be a trade off."

Leah thought about it a moment. "Yes. I think you're right." She checked her backpack. She had two clips for the Glock. "I'm going to fire off all but one clip. What do you think?"

Albert looked like he needed sleep. But Leah wanted his opinion before he slipped off. She said, "Well, I'm going to do some firing. When I'm done I want you to go to sleep and get some rest."

He nodded. She stepped away and began firing into the air in three round series, knowing that many considered this a signal. The local birds exploded skyward and some leaves came rustling down. When she was done, there was a certain amount of reverberating before the woods again went silent. She said to Albert, "Must be some hills nearby judging from those echoes." But he was already sound asleep.

She checked his bandage and covered him with his jacket before she herself stretched out.

Leah was asleep a while before something brought her awake. She leaped to her feet and reached for the Glock. A man dressed in a khaki uniform and a Smokey the Bear hat emerged from the woods. "Howdy, folks." He gazed into the lean-to and saw Albert's bloody bandage as the jacket only covered his torso. "I'm Ranger Rudge. Do you folks need help?"

"We sure do, Ranger. My friend here must have been hit by a hunter. He's hit in the leg."

Rudge leveled his gaze at them. "Hunters? No hunting season is in effect right now."

"I don't know," Leah said. Though the Ranger still looked dubious he got on his radio and called for help. About an hour later a four-wheel drive jeep arrived with another person, a woman. She went right to Albert and removed the bandage and checked his wound. With a slight frown on her face she retrieved a needle from her pack and loaded some drug into it.

As she inserted the needle into his arm, Leah asked, "How is he?"

"The wound is infected. He needs an antibiotic and a saline drip right away. I'm giving him the antibiotic now. As soon as we get him back to the ranger station I'll give him the drip."

It took them an hour to reach the station. When they arrived Ranger Rudge checked their IDs but still tended to veil a skeptical frown. Just before he left to check the IDs he said, "Please get your gun permit out for me to check."

"What are you going to do with my friend?"

Rudge said, "I'm going to have you folks airlifted out to Montpelier. The rangers there will have some more questions for you."

Leah was afraid of a bureaucratic foul up. She knew she could never convince anybody that Victor Luchensko was about to deliver a nuclear device to terrorists to be used against New York City.

The few rangers who manned the station were busy arranging for the helicopter medi-vac flight and tending to Albert. She waited for their attention to be even more diverted.

As soon as their attention was off of her, she slipped away and was off into the woods. Rudge had advised her that there was a road that connected with the Interstate just a couple of miles east of their station.

In twenty minutes or so she found a highway and thumbed a ride into Montpelier. She hated leaving Albert but at least she knew he was receiving medical attention.

Montpelier was the capitol of Vermont but it still wasn't a big town by big town standards. There was a municipal airport and she wondered if Victor used it to get to New York. She also wondered if he was able to get the device on board. After all, the whole idea of coming through the woods was to use private transportation to assure the authorities wouldn't get wind of the nuclear device.

She was dropped off downtown and took a cab to the nearest airline office, which was located in the lobby of the Montpelier Grande Hotel. There she learned that of the three commuter carriers flying to New York City none had left in the past three hours and two were scheduled within the hour. Maybe she had slipped in before the window shut. Perhaps he had to hike further than her but there he was, only a few feet away but totally unaware of her presence, trying to buy a ticket to New York. Would he be able to get it through? Should she shoot him right here and save the City of New York? And she thought, no doubt go to jail, regardless of his intentions.

She watched carefully as he sought to get the flight. But evidently there was some problem with the carry-on. She decided to call the cops. Let it all sort out later. She'd tell them what he has in his "carry-on."

She was at the phone bank busily checking instructions and inserting her credit card when she heard a familiar voice whisper in her ear. "Why, Leah. Funny to find you here?"

Slowly, she turned. She thought about going for the Glock. But when she turned his steely eyes told her it was too late for that. He was so close to her it was hard to see that he had a pistol aimed at her stomach. With the broad smile on his face there was little doubt to the passerby that they knew each other.

Speaking between tight teeth Victor fished in her pocket, found the Glock and slipped it into his own pocket. "Now," he said in a voice that was so saccharine that she could count the calories. "Come with me and remember, I have no need to keep you alive. If you give me any trouble I'll drop you where you stand."

She said nothing and offered no resistance, but her mind was whirling madly. He forced her to carry his boxed "carry-on" luggage and they headed for the check in counter of the hotel. In a few minutes, with her walking in front of him, he had registered them as man and wife and was given a room on the first floor. "My wife is afraid of heights," he said politely to the clerk.

Once in the room his smile disappeared. He said to her, "Lie down on the bed." Quickly he stripped off the pillow-cases, twisted them into ropes and secured her wrists to the bed headboard. He whipped off his belt and she blanched a bit, but he used it to secure her ankles together. She was grateful that he hadn't gagged her. In a few minutes she knew why. He began taunting her. "Do you think you were fooling me?" he asked.

"Actually I did," she said with a bit of a smirk.

"I was on to you from the beginning."

"Really?"

Now it was his turn to grin. "No, my dear. I'm lying. I wasn't on to you. I thought you really liked me."

"Maybe I do."

"Oh yes. And you're not playing Super Hero right now. Going to save the world."

"Maybe. Maybe I had something else in mind."

His brow raised. As much as he tried to hide it he was curious. "Such as?"

"Such as a piece of the action. I though maybe you could use me, but your men never gave me a chance to talk to you. They started blasting away."

"You can't be serious."

"I can't?"

"How do you know I didn't want the device to sell to the highest bidder?"

He barely veiled an evil smirk. "Now that I could respect. After all, money is what it is all about."

Victor leered at her with an evil grin. "But unfortunately, even if I have my way with you now, it wouldn't be as much fun as if you were an active participant. And after all, what do I need you for now. I'm afraid you are no longer useful, my dear." He approached her, unbuttoning his trousers.

Her eyes focused on his hands she said, "Are you sure you want it that way? I know some men like rape and forcing women, but I don't see you as one. Your ego is too big. Almost as big as your…"

He smiled broadly now. "So you remember."

"Of course. It would be hard to forget. Now do you want to hear my proposition or would you rather rape me while I lay here like a lump."

He sat on the edge of the bed. "You have my ear. What is your proposition?"

Chapter Twenty-Five

Victor Luchensko stared at his beautiful prisoner. There was no fear in her eyes. She was still haughty and her sexual dare turned him on and he decided not to rape her. Bluntly he asked her, "Okay, let's assume you're not just stalling to gain time. What is your proposition?"

She said, "I know how much you are getting from your connections."

"Indeed. And how do you know?"

"Doesn't matter. I know. You're getting two million American and safe passage out of town."

His brows raised. He said, "I'm impressed. And your proposition?"

"I can get nine million. Split that with me and you still have more than double your deal."

He scratched his chin and gazed at her. "And why should I believe you?"

"Why not? I'm at least as trustworthy as the scum you normally deal with."

He had to laugh outright at that. "You are so right my dear. It's too bad we can't be a team."

"Why can't we?" She grinned. "Look what we've been to each other."

He shook his head grinning all the time. "You are a lady after my own heart. I do wish I could believe you."

"Try me. What do you have to lose? If I'm lying you're no worse off, you get your two million and you're off to Rio. If I'm right, you get four and a half million. Of course you could try to stiff me, but if you do my deal part of the deal is I have to be free. And if I'm free you'll find me formidable."

"I believe that," he said. "What do I have to do to get you along with the deal."

"Be straight with me."

"That's all?"

"That's all I require of any man. That he be straight with me."

"My dear, you have me at a disadvantage."

"How's that?"

"I have had this feeling for sometime that you are leading me around by the nose. How can I trust you when I feel that you and that dead McAllister dude have pulled some type of con job on me."

"So why are we talking?"

He thought about that for a moment. "Good question. I guess you intrigue me. There's something about you that's so different than anyone I've ever known."

Victor surveyed her face for a while, trying to find some crack in her amour, but Leah's expression never changed.

Victor reached out and grabbed Leah by the chin, obviously enjoying the discomfort he was causing her. "I feel that you and your dead boyfriend are masters of deception. That you have perpetrated some type of scheme to deceive me so you could get close to me."

Squeezing her chin harder one last time he rose and walk to the table in the room, pouring himself a drink as he studied her. Raising his glass in a salute to her, he once again sat on the edge of the bed.

"If I ever figure out this scheme of you and your boyfriends, I will kill you, and I will enjoy doing it very very slowly......do I make myself clear."

Leah nodded her head before speaking.

"So? Do we have a deal?"

"Let me think about it. I'm going to check on my arrangements. I will no doubt be renting a car to drive to New York. The airlines want to check things and that's too risky."

He left and she slumped back on the bed. She didn't realize how the tension of the past forty-eight hours had wearied her. She was exhausted and was soon asleep. When she woke, the long shadows of early afternoon slanted into the room. She stretched and yawned realizing that her arms were now aching. The sleep was helpful but it also tended to overwhelm her. She seemed to be losing her spunk. Everything she had said to Victor was bravado, pure and simple. She had no connections. She was simply hoping to buy time and find a way to escape. She thought, Albert, I need you. You're my right arm. She lay there thinking. Her next thoughts turned to David. David, where are you? You've been around in the past to watch over me. Where are you now? I need you.

When Victor entered the room all thoughts turned to him. "Okay," he said. "How do we do your deal?"

She was actually relieved to see him. Now she had a chance to try to make something happen. "Simple," she said. "When we get to the city I call them. They've already agreed to pay me nine million for the device. They're part of a group that has more to gain than your guys. They so badly want to twist the beard of old Uncle Sam until it hurts. And this is going to make 9-11 look like a minor accident."

Both lapsed silent. Then she said, "Well? I need to get out of these damn bonds and get a shower."

That seemed to brighten him up. Silently he untied her. He didn't pull his weapon and so it seemed that they had a kind of a truce going on. Rubbing her wrists Leah headed for the shower.

She got into the shower, grateful that Victor hadn't followed her. She knew he expected sex but he seemed to be willing to wait for a better time.

He said, "Here's the deal. We leave right after dinner. We'll drive all night and be in the City in the morning. Now, how about some dinner?"

She said, "Great. I'm starving."

They dined on rare roast beef with all the trimmings. Then they got in the car that was waiting in the underground garage. Leah had wondered what the arrangements would be for the trip. Did he plan to tie her up and toss her in the back? When he didn't do that her spirits had picked up, until he handcuffed her to the door. That pretty much dashed her hopes of escape.

She had to keep up the game and couldn't let her guard down. So she didn't discourage him from talking. In fact, she encouraged him. He said, "You are unusual for an American woman."

"How so?"

"Well, the Mata Hari type is definitely not American. I know European and Middle Eastern women who will fit the role, but never an American."

"So you're only used to what kind of American women?"

"Party girls."

"Yes, I see you like the New York party scene."

He grinned. "Certainly."

"And what happens to women who cross you or displease you."

His face darkened. "What are you talking about?"

"Oh nothing. You just seem like a dangerous man."

"Maybe I am. Does that bother you?"

She didn't smile but leveled a cool gaze at him. "Au contraire."

He brightened again, sure he was getting closer to her.

They drove through the night stopping a couple of times for coffee. Leah wracked her brain but could think of no way to escape. Once they got to the city he would call her bluff and probably kill her outright.

At a truck stop in Poughkeepsie, New York, Victor went in for coffee. She asked for a large black. As a trucker walked by and ogled her she had an idea. She gestured to the man, a large burly guy with a beard, ponytail and a leather vest over a bare chest. Her gestures got his attention. She gestured for him to open the door. When he did he saw the handcuffs and his eyes popped. "Look," she said, "my boyfriend thinks he's cute keeping me cuffed till we get to New York. Could you lend me a pocket knife. I want to fix his ass." She knew if she asked him to get the cops he may or he may not and even if he did they probably would be long gone.

The guy said, "Jeez, lady. I don't want to interfere with any man's fun. I…"

"Please?" she said, batting her proverbial lids.

He gave her a goofy smirk and handed her the pocket knife. She quickly sawed through the leather of the car door and freed herself of it. "Gee thanks, Mister. You'll never know how much you've accomplished here today."

Looking sheepish he lumbered on his way.

As Victor returned a few moments later, Leah kept her right arm up, blocking his view of the sawed leather piece and pretending she was still bound to it. He handed her the coffee and sat down. She gestured to him to take off the lid. He put his own coffee down in the beverage holder and undid her large black coffee. He began to sip his coffee when Leah quickly dumped her whole cup on his lap. He screamed and reached for his genitals. As he did she reached into his jacket pocket and grabbed his pistol. She aimed it at him and fished in his other pocket for her Glock, which she found and stuffed in her waistband.

With no consideration for his pain she forced him out of the car. Leah stood him police fashion against the car, legs spread as she called the New York State Police on his cell phone. The scene drew the trucker back, curious as to what was happening. When he spoke to Leah she was distracted for a nanosecond and Victor lunged at her and grabbed the gun. As Leah struggled Victor cocked his fist and threw a punch connecting with her cheek. Victor leveled the gun at the slack jawed trucker and spat, "Get lost. This is none of your concern." The guy disappeared like smoke in the wind.

By the time Victor turned his attention back to Leah it was too late. From the ground she drew back her knee and lashed out in a straight-kneed kick that dropped him to the pavement. As he struggled to his feet Leah was already circling him like a cat in her Tae Kwan Do stance. The Russian staggered to his knees, but that was a far as he got. After a series of swing kicks and uppercuts, Victor lay on the pavement bleeding from the mouth and nose, struggling for breath.

The wail of the sirens in the distance was comforting and she knew he wasn't going to get up. She had one last taunt for him before the police arrived. "I'm gonna see to it that everybody at Attica knows you got beat up by a woman. That should make you somebody's girlfriend pretty quick."

Victor glared at her but behind the hatred, was genuine fear. He knew she was right. Five minutes later State Police cruisers surrounded their car. Leah showed them the device in the trunk and Homeland Security was immediately called. She gave the police detective who interviewed her Jonathan's name at the New York Police Department and that helped Leah escape a mountain of questions.

As she walked out of the State Police Headquarters out on the Interstate the sun was shining. Fast moving clouds had scudded by the sun and the sun had brightened the world. A soft breeze flipped her hair around. She tucked it behind her ear, in a quintessential feminine gesture and headed for her car and home.

EPILOGUE

Her svelte body was pure poetry. The clinging silk slip and perfectly fitted red bra shimmered in the subdued lighting before her dressing mirror as she raised her arms to run the brush through her long golden tresses. Her evening gown, haute couture in an understated way, hung in a nearby closet.

The hotel's elegance was evident in every corner of the suite. The lulling strains of Chopin filled the room in a muted way. It provided counterpoint to her even strokes as she applied lipstick and eyeliner. Her lovely face was revealed in the mirror in a dramatic way as her beauty reflected back into her green, cat-like eyes. She stole expectant glances in the mirror every so often, but her own image was all that she saw.

She was concentrating on her makeup again when a rather slim, stylish man dressed in polo garb appeared in the mirror, standing behind her. She whirled around and hurled a perfume bottle at him. It crashed into a paneled wall and clattered off in a noisy ricochet.

Her eyes widened as she surveyed the scene…there was nobody there. She watched in the mirror as he appeared once again, a shadow of her past once again returning. However, this time she knew it was different. She watched him as he bowed to her, his image clearly reflected in the mirror before her. She knew that this time was to be the last time she was to see him, that her contentment with the woman she had become would allow him to leave her forever.

"Good-bye David" was all she whispered as the shadow in the mirror faded away.

Leah had stayed in New York through-out Victors trial, waiting to see justice served. Unable to convict Victor on any charges related to the murdered girls, the District Attorney took satisfaction in the fact that Victor Luchensko was given a life sentence on the terrorism charges. Sitting in the court room with Brenda and Jonathon each day and then waiting for the jury's deliberations was the hardest part of this ordeal. But once the verdict was read, it was like a cloud was lifted from over Leah's head and she knew her new life in New York was about to begin.

As she finished dressing, she listened to the cd of Chopin, waiting for the alluring sound of the music to finish, bringing silence to the room. Waiting for a second, she wiped the tear from her eyes before crossing the room to the music center. She removed the disc from the player and placed it in it's case. This was David's favorite compact disc, it had traveled the world with him, bringing him comfort through the alluring sounds of the music. Leah gently placed the disc to her lips, kissing it before placing it on the shelf.

For Leah the elevator ride to the main lobby was like starting a new chapter of her life. For the first time since hearing of Alicia's murder, she knew that she had made the right choices in her life. As she stepped from the elevator into the lobby she marveled at it's transformation for tonight's upcoming New Year's Eve party. Since assuming control as management of the hotel, a role David never exercised, Leah had insisted that no expense was to be spared in ringing in the New Year.

Waiting in the lobby to greet her was Albert and Maria, once loyal employee's to David, now a couple with the rest of their lives ahead of them. Brenda was the first to marvel at her dress she had chosen for this evening affair, before introducing her date for the evening to Leah. It was the first time Leah had seen her look so happy since coming back to New York, obviously the guilty verdict Victor had received had brought contentment to her life. Jonathon waited for his turn to greet Leah, standing beside his wife Bobby, an obvious country girl transplanted into big city life. Hiding behind her father legs, Jonathon had to drag his little girl out from behind his legs. "This is Madison, our pride and joy. Maddy say hello to your aunt Leah."

Jonathon reached down and scooped up little Maddy in his arm before speaking to Leah. "Give her five minutes sitting beside you and you will know our whole life history. This ones a chatter box, we haven't found the switch yet to turn her off."

Leah reached out her arms to see if Maddy would come to her, surprised that she also extended her arms and hugged Leah. Tears welled in Leah's eyes as she knew she had found a new friend, holding her tightly as she crossed the room to the dining room. Asking everyone to be seated, she placed Maddy in a chair beside her before seating herself. Everyone was silent waiting for her to speak.

"Albert, if you would please do the evenings toast."

Standing, Albert waited until the waiter's filled all the glasses, "A toast to family and friends and to those who have gone on before us. May their journey be filled with as much happiness as we see in this room tonight. A special good-bye to my friend Bradley David McAllister, may he also find piece and happiness in his life until we meet again."

Leah watched as the food was being served, enjoying the sounds of chatter as laughter filled the room, listening to Matty each time she tugged on her sleeve. Leah was distracted when the hotel concierge approached her. "Ms Hammond, this note came for you, the gentleman said it was urgent."

Briefly scanning the note Leah was obviously concerned, "Where is the man that brought this note"

"I'm sorry Ms Hammond, the gentlemen left as soon as I took the note from him."

Sitting still, Leah felt the tugging of the sleeve once again, lowering her head as Maddy said she had something to ask her. Her laughter rang loud as she hugged Matty, pondering her question on why the man from the lobby seemed to be such a happy funny guy. All eyes were on her as she simply stated, "From the mouths of babes..."

Her gauze sought out Albert, her eyes telling him she needed him. Meeting him at the entrance to the lobby she watched as he to read the note then allowed his gauze to survey the lobby before speaking.

"Hopefully video surveillance got a good glimpse of who dropped off this note to the front desk. But lets wait until tomorrow to worry about this, go back and be with your family tonight.. I will handle this matter myself."

Albert watched as Leah crossed the room and rejoined Maddy at the table. He knew by the way both held hands that Leah had made a friend for life, something she needed most of all. He read the note once again as he studied the lobby.

It simply stated.......

I know who you are and what you have done...and for that you shall be FOREVER DAMMED

New York's finest.......

Novel cover design by Acer Graphics...India www.acergraphics.com

Back Cover Design
(Picture of Author) -Merdick Earl McFarlane- with permission by Ilija Galic C/O Love Unlimited Studio 1032 Lasalle Blvd Sudbury Ontario 705-566-9595

Enter our on-line contest for Master of Deception...CAN YOU FIND THE NAMES OF MERDICK EARL McFARLANE'S NEXT TWO NOVELS. RE-READ THE LAST TWO CHAPTERS OF THIS NOVEL.
BURIED IN THESE CHAPTERS ARE THE NEW NOVEL TITLES. ENTER YOUR GUESS ON-LINE AT www.mcfarlanemediagroup.com CONTEST RUNS FROM APRIL 1 2007 TO DECEMBER 31, 2007.... ONE WINNER WILL BE SELECTED FROM ALL THE CORRECT ENTRIES TO WIN THE CONTEST. Enter for your chance to win $250.00 USD.

Or enter on line to be one of the Characters in the Next Leah Hammond Sequel. All character descriptions are also available on line at www.mcfarlanemediagroup.com. Contest closes September 30, 2007

ISBN 1425108865